LUMINANCE AND RESONANCE

LHYNDZY

To my Dad in heaven, your wisdom and love continue to guide me. I hope I've made you proud.

To my Mom, for your endless love and sacrifices.

To my Aunt, who recently left us, your spirit lives on in every word I write.

To my brothers, the steadfast constants in an ever-changing world.

And to a few, but invaluable friends — who give without expecting anything in return.

Your unconditional support means the world to me.

This book is a tribute to the love, lessons, and legacy you've all given me.

1

The Discovery of Auras

McKhynzy, known to her friends as Khynzy, had always known that the world around her was more than what meets the eye. Colours, hues, and shades swirled like gentle currents, casting a unique glow around people and other living things.

When she was six, sitting on her child-sized art table in her room, sketchbook open before her, she realised that not everyone could see the radiant colours that danced around each person.

Gripping her coloured pencils with tiny, chubby fingers, Khynzy focused on her parents, who sat on the couch, engrossed in a grown-up conversation. Her mom's aura was a calming shade of blue mixed with streaks of purple, reflecting her nurturing and wise nature. Her dad's aura was a deep shade of blue with golden edges, symbolising his wisdom and unwavering stability.

Feeling a burst of excitement, Khynzy picked a purple pencil for her mom's aura and a blue one for her dad's, adding touches of gold as her small hands could manage. Soon, her drawing was full of these shades, making her parents look like they were glowing. When she showed her parents the drawing, they looked confused.

"Sweetie," her mother began, her brow furrowed, "Why did you colour around us like that?" her mom asked.

"You can't see it?" Khynzy said, surprised.

Her dad smiled. "No, we can't. Looks like you can see special things."

"But why?" Khynzy asked, confused.

"Can you see these colours on other people too?" her mom asked.

"Yeah, everybody has them!" Khynzy answered.

Her dad leaned in, curious. "What do these colours mean?"

"The colours change when people are happy or sad," Khynzy explained.

Her mother smiled softly, reaching out to place a hand on Khynzy's. "Zee-zee, those colours are called auras. It sounds like a special gift, sweetheart. Just remember, not everyone will see things the way you do."

Her dad nodded. "It's like your own secret, okay?"

Concerned but fascinated by their daughter's unique experience, her parents decided it was time for a professional opinion. "We should probably take you to an eye doctor just to make sure everything's okay," her mom suggested.

Having conducted extensive tests, the eye doctor turned to Khynzy's parents with a reassuring smile. "Khynzy's eyes are in excellent condition; I couldn't find any issues. However, the ability she has described—seeing auras—is something that doesn't fall under the scope of eye health or vision issues. Medically, her vision is completely normal. I would recommend consulting with a few other specialists to get a comprehensive understanding, perhaps starting with a neurologist. They might be able to provide more insight into this unique phenomenon."

Taking the doctor's advice to heart, her parents took her to various specialists, from neurologists to psychologists.

Despite multiple evaluations and even more tests, no one could explain Khynzy's unique ability. Each expert concluded that there was nothing medically wrong with her, deepening the mystery surrounding her gift.

The validation from her parents and the lack of a medical explanation were both comforting and weighty for Khynzy. She had a unique gift, and with it came the unspoken understanding that she would use it wisely.

One day at school, a minor incident occurred that would put Khynzy's unique ability to the test. During recess, she noticed that her classmate Frank's favourite toy had gone missing. The classroom was in chaos as Frank frantically searched for his toy, his aura shifting from excitement to distress.

As she looked around, Khynzy saw one colour that didn't look right. It was all jumbled and nervous.

"I think I know where the toy is," Khynzy told her teacher, Mrs. Robertson.

"How do you know?" Mrs. Robertson asked, her eyebrows knitting together in curiosity and slight concern.

"I saw colours that looked funny," Khynzy said, trying to make her unique ability sound simple.

"Colours?" Mrs Robertson paused, looking puzzled but intrigued.

Mrs Robertson checked the bag of the student whose aura Khynzy had found suspicious. Sure enough, there lay Frank's toy. As Mrs. Robertson sorted out the situation, she gave Khynzy a thoughtful look as if storing away a puzzle to be solved later.

As the teacher addressed the situation, Khynzy felt a mix of relief and satisfaction. Her ability to read auras had helped her unravel the mystery without directly accusing anyone. It was a subtle way to make a difference, to see beyond the surface and understand the emotions that often remained hidden.

As the day faded into evening, Khynzy sat by her window, gazing at the world outside. The colours of the world remained a vibrant tapestry unseen by most. Yet, in that moment, she felt a newfound sense of wonder and connection to the world around her. Like whispered secrets, auras painted the canvas of her reality, a reminder of the beauty that existed beyond the visible.

2

The Shattered Sky

As Khynzy's parents prepare for their overseas business trip, Khynzy watched them with a mix of excitement and apprehension, knowing that this journey was necessary for their work but also dreading their departure. Standing beside her was her Aunt Mildred, her father's sister, whose aura usually shone with a blend of rich oranges and soothing lavenders, symbolising her zest for life and comforting presence.

"Don't worry, Zee-zee," Aunt Mildred said, gently squeezing her shoulder. "Your parents will be fine, and I'll be right here with you until they return."

Her mother bent down to fasten Khynzy's shoelaces. "You take care while we're away, sweetheart," she said, her eyes filled with maternal love. "We won't be gone long, and we'll bring you a special gift for your 11th birthday."

Khynzy nodded, her young heart heavy with a sense of unease she couldn't explain. She glanced at her father, a strong and supportive figure with an aura that usually radiated shades of blue. Today, though, his aura was tinged with black, an unusual departure from his usual reassuring presence.

"Dad," Khynzy began hesitantly, "are you sure everything will be okay? I don't like how your auras look today; they keep changing from blue to black."

Her father knelt and hugged her tightly. "Sweetheart, sometimes grown-ups have to do things that may seem a little scary, but it's all part of our job. We promise to be careful, and we'll be back before you know it."

Tears welled up in Khynzy's eyes, and she clung to her parents, feeling a growing sense of dread. "I'm going to miss you so much," she whispered.

Her mother gently wiped away her tears. "We'll miss you too, Zee-zee. But we'll call you every day, and you'll see how fast the time flies."

❦

At the airport, Khynzy stood beside her parents and Aunt Mildred as they checked in their luggage. She couldn't shake the feeling that something was wrong, her anxiety growing with each step they took away from her.

She couldn't hold back her fear any longer. "Mom, Dad, something's wrong! Your auras—they keep changing. That's not right!"

Her parents exchanged concerned glances and knelt to her eye level. Her father's voice quivered as he reassured her, "Zee-zee, we love you so much. Remember that, no matter what. We'll be back soon."

Tears streamed down Khynzy's cheeks as she hugged them tightly, her intuition screaming that something terrible was about to happen. She didn't want to let go, but eventually, they had to board the plane.

Khynzy felt a knot in her stomach as she watched her parents disappear toward their departure gate. Turning to Aunt Mildred, she asked with an anxious voice, "Can we wait until their plane takes off, Aunt Mildred?"

Understanding Khynzy's need for reassurance, Aunt Mildred nodded. "Of course, sweetheart. We'll stay right here."

They found seats with a clear view of the runway, and Aunt Mildred pulled out her phone, navigating to a flight tracking app. "Let's keep an eye on their flight," she said, reassuringly smiling.

As they waited, Khynzy's phone buzzed with a message from her mom: "We're about to take off. Love you lots!"

"Love you too, Mom. Safe flight," Khynzy responded, her fingers trembling.

Her dad's text followed shortly after: "See you soon, munchkin. Be good for Aunt Mildred."

"I will, Dad. Love you," she replied, fighting back tears.

They watched the departure board intently, and after a few tense moments, her parents' flight status changed to 'Departed'. Khynzy felt a mixture of relief and lingering worry.

But then, a loud explosion rang out, jolting everyone in the terminal. Panic ensued as people rushed to the windows, staring at the plume of smoke rising in the distance.

Khynzy's heart sank, and she turned to Aunt Mildred, her eyes wide with fear. "Aunt Mildred, was that their plane?"

Looking at her phone, Aunt Mildred saw that the flight status had not changed. She shook her head, her voice filled with disbelief, "No, no, it can't be. Their plane just took off. It's too soon."

However, as the minutes ticked by, the grim reality became apparent. The news spread quickly through the airport, confirming the devastating event. Khynzy's parents' flight had ended in tragedy.

Aunt Mildred pulled Khynzy close, her heart breaking as they faced the tragic reality together.

In the days that followed, Khynzy's heart ached with grief and loss. She missed her parents terribly and wished she could turn back time and hold on to them just a little longer.

Her gift of seeing auras, once a source of wonder, had now become a heavy burden, forever linked to the memory of that fateful day.

Aunt Mildred, who had been with Khynzy through this ordeal, became her source of strength and comfort. With no children of her own, Aunt Mildred became fully committed to caring for Khynzy in her parents' absence. It was a bittersweet arrangement, one that forged a deeper bond between aunt and niece.

As she grew older, Khynzy would use her abilities to bring understanding and solace to others. Still, the pain of losing her parents and the vivid auras of that day would remain a part of her, a reminder of the fragility of life and the darkness that sometimes shrouded even the brightest of auras.

3

The Mosaic of Auras

Khynzy's smart home device chirped insistently, filling the room with its synthetic voice. "It's 6:30 a.m., rise and shine, genius at work," it announced. She groaned, muttering, "Snooze," without opening her eyes, and sank back into her duvet.

Nine minutes later, the device was at it again. This time, she mumbled, "Fine, fine," clearly not eager to leave her cosy nest. And then she blurted, "Snooze," in a slightly louder voice so the device could hear.

By the third announcement, Khynzy knew there was no escaping the inevitable. "Alright, I get it. Stop," she mumbled, commanding the device to cease its alarms as she swung her legs over the side of the bed.

As she sat up, her eyes scanned her room, landing on her collection of succulents sitting on the windowsill. Their auras were a calming blend of green and yellow, emitting a sense of resilience and a positive, uplifting energy. She preferred succulents—they were the only plants she managed to keep alive.

Today's outfit was far from the hoodies, graphic tees, and sneakers commonly associated with software developers.

Instead, she buttoned up a long-sleeved white shirt and slipped into a blue and white plaid sleeveless dress. As she tied a white bow neatly at the collar of her shirt, her grey eyes met her reflection and the subtle aura that danced around it— a gentle palette of pastel colours, a reflection of her calm demeanour and sense of peace.

With a touch of minimal makeup and a few quick curls at the ends of her medium-brown hair, she was almost ready. She opted for white brogues today, which perfectly tied her preppy ensemble together.

After packing her laptop into her bag, she realised something was missing: her ID lanyard. Where had she left it? Then it hit her — she'd gone straight to her soundproof drum room last Friday, still wearing her ID. She'd taken it off and left it near the hi-hat. With a sigh, she retrieved it before heading out, locking the door behind her.

As she stepped out of her cosy apartment with her laptop bag in hand, she couldn't help but feel that something extraordinary awaited her, as it did every day — the ever-shifting tapestry of auras.

The city came alive as she made her way to the train station. The streets bustled with people from all walks of life, and each person emitted a unique aura, a shimmering halo of colours that reflected their thoughts, emotions, and the dynamics of their interactions.

Some auras were warm and inviting, bathed in hues of gold and soft blues. These belonged to individuals who felt content and at peace with the world. Lovers shared intimate moments, their auras dancing harmoniously with shades of pink and passionate red.

Conversely, those consumed by anger or frustration emanated fiery auras, a palette of reds and oranges. Their emotions blazed like an uncontrolled wildfire.

Khynzy observed a stranger's aura shift from a soothing

green to a vivid shade of yellow when a friendly passerby struck up a conversation. A family sharing a meal nearby radiated a collective aura of vibrant blues, representing the harmony they found in each other's company.

As she entered the station, her eyes were drawn to a man with a brilliant, shimmering blue aura that extended around him like a protective shield. To her, this shade of blue signified profound inner peace amidst the world's chaos and the serenity radiated from him.

Close to the serene man stood a group of chattering teenagers, their auras dancing with vibrant shades of orange and yellow. Khynzy understood this combination well; it was the enthusiasm of youth mixed with creativity. They were on a journey together, and their auras were a testament to their boundless energy and zest for life.

The train station itself was a symphony of auras. Commuters exuded a spectrum of colours, mirroring their thoughts about the impending workday. Some, filled with enthusiasm for their jobs, shone in bright, optimistic auras. Others, burdened by stress or unhappiness, cast a gloomy shadow around them.

What fascinated Khynzy the most was how these auras interacted. As people brushed past each other, their auras intertwined, briefly blending or clashing in a dance of emotions. A moment of kindness could soften a harsh aura, while a heated argument could ignite fiery sparks.

4

The Unspoken Gift

Seconds before his alarm was set to go off, Levi's eyes flicked open. A practised internal clock had him waking up just in time as if to assert some level of control over his day. He silenced the alarm before it had the chance to disturb the morning quiet.

Today's outfit was a tailored dark grey blazer, crisp white shirt, and black trousers. Unlike many in his field who leaned toward hoodies and sneakers, Levi chose smart-casual attire as his workday armour. Although on Fridays, he allowed himself the luxury of casual clothes, a concession to the end-of-week vibe.

Buttoning up his shirt, his eyes wandered to his guitar leaning against the wall. It was an instrument he played for fun, a personal retreat from the complex algorithms and codes that defined his professional life. Levi took a moment to ponder the significance of the day. He was starting at a new company as a software architect, stirring a blend of excitement and apprehension.

After adding a final touch with a splash of cologne, he grabbed his leather laptop bag and headed out.

For a moment, he considered taking his car to work. It

would be more convenient and less crowded, but he decided against it. Today, he felt a strange urge to take the train instead. He could not quite explain why, but something drew him to the bustling platform of the train station.

Levi felt a familiar sensation settling in as he made his way through the morning crowds. It was a unique gift he had possessed for as long as he could remember — one that set him apart from others. He owned an extraordinary and, at times, burdensome ability. He could hear the unspoken, negative or malicious thoughts of those around him as clearly as if they were spoken aloud. It was not a gift he had ever asked for, nor one he particularly enjoyed.

In a world where thoughts were often kept private, this gift had been both a blessing and a curse. It allowed him to see through people's facades to understand their true intentions, but it also exposed him to the depths of human darkness.

And that was not the extent of his unusual talent. Levi had another, even more unsettling ability. He could 'whisper' suggestions back into their minds. It was not always malevolent, but it was not always benevolent either. It was a double-edged sword that had caused him more dilemmas than he cared to admit. Most times, this was to guide them toward better choices. But he had to admit, on a few occasions, he'd used it to tip the scales in his favour. But Levi had transformed. Once tempted to use his powers for ill, he had consciously decided to be a force for good. Nowadays, he uses his extraordinary abilities to sow seeds of positivity in a world often clouded by negativity.

As he walked toward the train station, Levi allowed himself to tap into this unusual ability. It was as if he was tuning in to the collective consciousness of the morning commuters. He could sense their worries, insecurities, and hidden desires.

Levi noticed a mother from afar, pushing a stroller, her face portraying exhaustion. As he walked by, he heard the piercing thoughts of inadequacy reverberating loudly, *I'm never enough..., I'm failing them..., I can't do this right...* These were intertwined with a torrent of stress and worry;* So much to do... The bills... No time...I'm so tired...*, each a heavy load on her already burdened soul. Without approaching, Levi whispered gentle reassurances into her chaotic mind: *You're doing well... Take a moment for yourself...* Her shoulders relaxed slightly, the relentless circle of self-doubt interrupted, permitting a moment of contemplation for her own well-being.

Further down the street, he crossed paths with a harried-looking businessman. The man's thoughts were a storm of anxiety, *I'm going to mess up... They'll see right through me... I'm not cut out for this...*, each drowning him more deeply in a sea of self-doubt and worry. Sensing the overwhelming negative spiral, Levi whispered a beacon of hope into the man's turbulent mind, suggesting, *You have the knowledge... Trust in your capabilities...* The businessman's tense expression began to morph, shadows of self-assurance replacing the fears as he steadied his resolve and regained his composure.

As he neared the train station, he spotted a young girl sitting on a bench, her eyes swollen from tears. Her thoughts were a heartbreaking symphony of loneliness, *I'm all alone... Nobody understands... I'm invisible to the world...*, each note resounding with the pain of isolation and despair. Sensing her desolation, Levi whispered words of encouragement into her shattered spirit, gently urging, *Find someone you trust... Share your pain....* The girl wiped away her tears, a newfound resolve to seek help shining through her sorrowful eyes.

As Levi entered the lift going up to the train's platform, he couldn't help but marvel at the power he held within him, a power that could shape the thoughts and decisions of those he encountered. It was a double-edged gift, one that came with a weighty responsibility.

5

The Omen in the Lift

As the lift ascended, Levi honed in on the thoughts of those trapped with him, orchestrating a symphony of darkness. Among the passengers was one man, an employee of the railway company. This employee harboured a grievance, festering over years of perceived injustices, and today, he had hatched a plot to sabotage the train service.

Levi's heart raced as he realised the potential harm this could cause innocent commuters. He whispered into the man's thoughts, *Perhaps revenge isn't the answer. I understand your frustration, but there are other ways to address your concerns. Hurting innocent people won't solve anything.*

The man blinked, momentarily bewildered by the unfamiliar voice in his head. He glanced around, finding no one who seemed privy to his inner turmoil. He refocused on the voice guiding his thoughts.

Consider this, Levi continued, *what if you exposed their misdeeds, not through chaos, but through truth? Become an advocate for change, a symbol of justice.*

The man's clenched fist began to relax as he pondered the alternative path suggested by the mysterious voice. By the time the lift reached the floor before the train platform, he was no longer plotting revenge; he was contemplating a more righteous course of action.

The lift doors slid open, revealing Khynzy's intention to board. She possessed a unique ability to see auras, and her gift had saved her from trouble many times before. However, as she stood there, her gaze flitting from one passenger to another, hesitation overcame her. The dark, shadowy auras surrounding the people inside sent chills down her spine, save for one man, who appeared devoid of any aura.

The dark aura that enveloped the other passengers was not the vibrant, lively hues she had grown accustomed to seeing. Instead, they were an abyss of inky blackness, a void that seemed to swallow the very essence of life itself.

Her intuition screamed at her to stay out of that confined space. She hesitated, her hand hovering over the lift button, her gaze locked onto the man with shockingly blue eyes but no aura. Panic surged through Khynzy as she stepped back, her fingers trembling, choosing not to step into the lift. Levi, noticing her reluctance, made the split-second decision to exit the lift alongside her.

At a loss for what to say to warn the others without sounding suspicious, Khynzy watched in silent horror as the lift doors slid shut, sealing the fate of those inside. Her mind raced to find an explanation, but panic left her grasping for words.

Just moments later, as they exchanged meaningful glances filled with unspoken questions, a loud explosion reverberated from within the lift. It startled Levi and Khynzy and the nearby passengers waiting for their turn, scattering them in fear as shockwaves surged through the corridor.

Levi and Khynzy shared a bewildered and concerned look. The bustling train station had transformed into a scene of devastation. Emergency responders raced toward the epicentre of the catastrophe as passengers scrambled for safety. Something had gone wrong inside that lift, and whatever it was, they were both grateful not to have been a part of it.

☙

Khynzy, ensconced in her warm apartment, remained fixated on the television screen as the news anchor solemnly declared, "We return with a pivotal update on the horrifying lift incident at Redwood Station."

A cold shiver permeated her as the memories of chaotic auras surrounding the lift resurfaced, their darkness making her rethink, ultimately choosing not to step inside. The reporter, Blake Carson, conveyed the latest findings, "Investigators have determined that an explosive device, detonating prematurely, caused the explosion. It wasn't an accident as earlier believed."

"A bomb," Khynzy murmured, her emotions a torrent of relief interwoven with sorrow. While thankful for her forewarning gift, she wondered about those less fortunate; had they sensed any impending danger?

☙

Elsewhere in the city, Levi, in his secluded abode, had been anxiously traversing through channels until the detailed news update arrested his attention. "Finally, some clarity," he pondered, the morning's harrowing memories still vivid. He was there amidst a sea of negative thoughts, one, in particular, resonating with menacing intentions—a man plotting a sinister disruption to the train service.

At that crucial moment, Levi infused whispers of empathy into the man's conscience. The man's demeanour changed; his gaze became distant before reflecting a softer reality. A relieved Levi exited the lift, but then catastrophe struck unexpectedly.

Blake Carson continued with a grave tone, "This incident wasn't mere misfortune; it was an act of sabotage that, had it not occurred prematurely, could have resulted in a tragedy of much greater proportions."

Levi sat there, drowning in guilt, relief, and regret. His subtle intervention may have prevented an evil act, but it did not halt the subsequent tragedy that unfolded.

6

A Name Without Vowels

Levi, being a recent addition to the Tech squad, found himself in a bind as he navigated through various team collaboration tools, trying desperately to get in touch with 'Mackenzie' from the Code squad. His manager and the lead architect, who had instructed him to collaborate with her, were out of the office, making it even more challenging to confirm he was reaching out to the right person. Frustration mounting, Levi decided to take a short break, hoping to clear his head. As he went to the kitchen for a glass of water, still ruminating over how to find Mackenzie, he unexpectedly collided with a colleague, momentarily pulling him out of his work-related contemplation.

"Whoa, sorry about that," Levi said as he steadied himself.

Then his eyes met hers. Recognition flashed in Levi's eyes. "Wait a minute. We've met before, haven't we? Weren't we almost in that train station lift that exploded?"

Khynzy's eyes widened. "Oh, that's right! It's you! The lift accident we narrowly escaped. Talk about grim yet unforgettable first meeting."

Levi nodded solemnly. "Indeed, a rather explosive one, if I may say so. By the way, I'm Levi Echo Moonstrider from the

Tech squad. I've been on a wild goose chase across various collaboration tools trying to get in touch with Mackenzie from the Code squad, but I couldn't find that name anywhere. Are you, by any chance, Mackenzie?"

Wearing a warm smile, the young woman before him replied, "Yes and no. My name is McKhynzy, M-C-K-H-Y-N-Z-Y, not the usual 'Mackenzie' spelling, which might be why you had trouble finding me on those platforms. But I am indeed from the Code squad."

Levi raised an eyebrow in amused disbelief. "McKhynzy, that's quite a unique name. Did your parents have an aversion to vowels or something?"

Khynzy chuckled, her eyes sparkling with delight. "You wouldn't believe how many times I've heard that one," grinning, she added, "wait till you hear my last name."

"Alright, hit me." Levi encouraged.

"It's Skylyght, S-K-Y-L-Y-G-H-T, no vowels there either."

Levi couldn't help himself; he burst into laughter. "McKhynzy Skylyght! Your parents really must have had some kind of vendetta against vowels. But I must say, it's a name I won't forget."

Levi couldn't help but ask, "By the way, should I call you McKhynzy, or is there a nickname you prefer?"

Khynzy smiled and replied, "Most people just call me Khynzy. You can too if you'd like."

As they continued chatting and walking down the hallway, Levi realised that sometimes, the most unexpected encounters could brighten even the most mundane workdays, especially when working with colleagues who shared unusual experiences was on the horizon. Curious as to why he could not hear any thoughts from Khynzy, he made a mental note to remember her unique name, McKhynzy Skylyght.

Meanwhile, Khynzy's gaze unconsciously scanned for

Levi's aura, a habit she had developed over the years. She had first noticed the strange absence of his aura during their brief encounter at the train station, a missing element that had stayed with her. Now, walking beside him, she was again struck by the void where his aura should be. The consistent absence deepened the enigma surrounding him and fanned her curiosity.

When they approached the end of the hallway, Levi glanced at his watch and realised it was almost lunchtime. "Hey, since it's nearly lunch, would you be interested in grabbing a bite together? We could also discuss our collaboration project," he suggested, hoping to spend more time with Khynzy and dive into the work ahead.

Khynzy's eyes lit up at the invitation. "Sure, I'd love to. It's a great opportunity to get to know my new collaborator," she agreed.

As they made their way toward the cafe, Levi couldn't help but admire Khynzy's vibrant sense of style, a mix of professionalism and creative flair that caught his eye. Likewise, Khynzy noted Levi's well-tailored attire and the confidence with which he carried himself. Both felt an unspoken mutual appreciation for each other's physical appearance as they walked, adding a subtle layer of excitement to their impending lunch and work collaboration.

7

The Emotional Code

On Wednesday morning, Khynzy settled into her ergonomic chair, its cushion moulding perfectly to her posture. She was toggling between her work and her unique gift—observing the auras that enveloped her colleagues when Stella, their squad's user interface designer, breezed into Khynzy's workspace, her energy as vibrant as ever. "Hey Khynzy, how's it going? I've just seen the latest episode of that K-Drama I told you about—you have to catch up!"

Khynzy looked up, instantly captivated by the swirl of colours that made up Stella's aura. Vibrant blues and greens still dominated, signifying her creativity and empathy, but today, they were tinged with flashes of bright pink and orange, colours that screamed enthusiasm and excitement—so fitting for a K-Drama aficionado.

"I promise I will! Just need to finish this code, then I'm all in," Khynzy said, minimising her work momentarily.

Stella pulled up a chair beside Khynzy's desk, sipping herbal tea from the office kitchen. "Take your time, but know you're missing out on some quality drama and romance!"

As Stella spoke, Khynzy noticed a flicker of lavender in her friend's aura—a nuance she hadn't seen before. Lavender usually indicates depth and wisdom. "You seem different today, more... insightful? What's new?" Khynzy ventured.

Stella laughed, her eyes twinkling. "Oh, you think so? I've been diving into some new UX courses. Plus, the complexities of K-Drama relationships are really making me think!"

Khynzy chuckled. "I bet they are!"

Despite their differences—Stella's flair for design, her love for K-dramas, and Khynzy's structured world of coding—their auras meshed perfectly. It was like an unspoken language of colours and energies that only Khynzy could perceive. She felt grateful for this friendship, one of the few where she could be her full self—even if that meant keeping her unique ability a secret.

As Stella returned to her desk, Khynzy's gaze moved across the room, taking in the colours that told her more about her coworkers than any online resume ever could. For most, their auras were soothing, calming pastels and bright primary hues, reflecting their general good intentions and straightforward personalities.

But Jennie's aura was different. It swirled with a murky mix of green and brown, resembling the storm clouds that loom ominously, even on a perfectly sunny day. Khynzy had long suspected Jennie harboured ill feelings toward her, and her aura was all the confirmation she needed.

"Hey, Khynzy, I noticed you've been deeply engrossed in the encryption algorithm," Jennie began, leaning casually against Khynzy's desk. Her voice was tinged with a sweetness that didn't reach her eyes. "Seems complex. Need any help?"

Khynzy glanced up, her face lighting up with a practised smile. "I appreciate the offer, Jennie. It's kind of you to ask. But I think I've got it under control."

Jennie's eyes narrowed for a fraction of a second. "Well, remember, we're a team here. No need to be a lone wolf. Just holler if you find yourself out of your depth."

Khynzy nodded, "Will do, thanks."

As Jennie walked away, Khynzy didn't miss the eye-roll that Jennie thought she'd hidden. Her aura flared a venomous red before settling into its usual stormy colours. Khynzy shook her head and sighed, already anticipating the next round.

During the weekly team meeting, Jennie sat diagonally opposite Khynzy, perfectly positioned to catch the eye of their technical lead, Dan. Throughout the meeting, Jennie threw subtle jabs cleverly disguised as constructive feedback.

"Khynzy, that backend integration you've been working on —how confident are you in its efficiency?" Jennie's eyebrow shot up, her voice laden with faux concern.

Khynzy leaned back in her chair, calculating her response. "I've done multiple tests, and the results have been promising. I'm confident it meets the project requirements."

Post-meeting, Khynzy couldn't help but observe Jennie. She was now speaking with Dan, animatedly discussing a new project idea. Her aura shifted, now radiating a vibrant yellow tinged with streaks of dark brown—the colour of ambition marred by deception.

Later in the afternoon, Khynzy reviewed the team's code and stumbled upon an error in Jennie's section. The bug was not just a minor oversight; it could compromise the system's security. Grappling with the ethical dilemma, she weighed whether to inform Jennie personally or bring it up during the daily standup meeting; she was concerned that addressing it in their meeting could embarrass her colleague.

Opting to approach Jennie directly, she walked over to her desk. "I discovered a security loophole in your code. Mind if I show you?"

Jennie's aura shifted dramatically, revealing her true emotional turmoil. "Why, certainly. Teach me, O wise one," she said, sarcasm veiling her voice.

Together, they debugged the error. Jennie's aura oscillated between shades of grey and deep red—embarrassment and anger fighting for dominance.

"Thanks for catching that," Jennie finally muttered, her aura settling into a dark, cloudy grey.

Khynzy nodded and returned to her desk, her aura swirling in a complex dance of purples and blues, the colours of wisdom and intuition. As she resumed work, she reflected on the complex tapestry of human emotions and intentions, wondering if her unique gift was a blessing or a curse.

8

Unwritten Code

Jennie's eyes darted between her dual monitors and the scene unfolding to her right. Khynzy was laughing with Levi, a recently-joined software architect around Jennie's age, about 24. Despite his youth, Levi's talent and experience were undeniable, quickly earning him the respect of colleagues from various squads. The aura of camaraderie around them seemed almost palpable, fuelling Jennie's recurring sense of jealousy.

Two years older than Khynzy, Jennie had always taken pride in her professional competence. Even though she had been in the field longer, she couldn't deny Khynzy's rapid rise in just two years since she started coding. In terms of technical prowess, Jennie considered herself more seasoned, but Khynzy's knack for analytical troubleshooting made her one of the top developers in the company. Yet it wasn't just her professional skills that stood out. Khynzy had a certain allure that drew people to her for her technical acumen and effortless charm. Meanwhile, Jennie, often immersed in the depths of code and logic, struggled to connect similarly. And while Khynzy's natural beauty was undeniable, Jennie couldn't help but feel overshadowed.

A flashback from a couple of days ago crossed Jennie's mind. She had tried to publicly outshine Khynzy by offering to help her with complex coding, insinuating that she could solve what Khynzy could not. The plan backfired spectacularly. Khynzy found a glaring mistake in Jennie's code and told her privately, saving her the embarrassment of a public callout. The courtesy stung, mainly because Jennie wasn't sure she would have been as gracious if the roles were reversed.

Levi, who had the unusual ability to sense negative thoughts, looked toward Jennie and caught her eye. "You look extremely focused, Jennie. Working on something big?"

Startled, she looked up. "Uh, yes, just trying to iron out some bugs," she said, realising how engrossed she had been.

Levi nodded knowingly. "It's good to be diligent, but don't forget to come up for air. When was the last time you took a break?"

"Been meaning to," Jennie said, feeling a bit self-conscious. "Just haven't had a chance yet."

Levi's eyes twinkled, almost as if he understood more than he let on. "Why don't we all head to the cafe down the block? We could use a change of scenery, and their coffee is stellar." He gestured to the door, Stella and Khynzy nodding in agreement. "We're discussing a new cross-squad project, and your perspective, Jennie, would be invaluable."

Jennie hesitated, taking a moment to register the invite. It was a chance, not only professionally but socially. "Alright," she agreed, "I could use a break, and I'm intrigued by the project."

As they made their way to the cafe, the ambience shifted from the formality of the office to the casual clinking of cups and murmurs of conversations. They settled into a booth, Levi and Stella on one side, Khynzy and Jennie on the other.

As they delved into the project details, Jennie found herself more and more engaged. However, during a lull in the conversation, Khynzy turned to her, "You know, your ideas align with mine. It's amazing how similar our approaches are."

Jennie looked into Khynzy's sincere eyes and realised something profound. All this time, she had cast Khynzy as a rival in her mind, but this self-imposed competition had only held her back, limiting her perspectives and narrowing her possibilities. Collaboration, not competition, might be the way forward. She had the technical skills; what she needed was to cultivate the soft skills, the emotional intelligence that seemed to come so naturally to Khynzy. It was time for a new approach—not just to coding but to her complex emotional algorithms.

Returning Khynzy's smile, Jennie replied, "I think we could make a great team." And as the afternoon wore on, the possibilities began to unfold.

As they continued discussing the cross-squad project, Jennie felt her initial apprehension morph into cautious optimism. Here was her chance to shine and contribute in ways beyond lines of code. Maybe she could also learn something about that elusive quality called "charm."

And so, as they delved into project specifics, Jennie also stepped into a new, unfamiliar role. She was not just a software developer with a chip on her shoulder but a team player eager to learn and contribute.

9

A Game of Auras

With the final minutes of the workweek ticking away, Stella leaned over her desk and shot Khynzy a mischievous smile. "Hey, how about we shake things up this weekend?"

Khynzy looked up from her laptop, intrigued. "What do you have in mind?"

"How about a poker night at the new casino downtown this Saturday? I've heard you're quite the poker player." Stella persisted. "I've been curious to see if you're as good as the rumours suggest. Is it skill, or was it just beginner's luck?"

Khynzy chuckled. "I've won a few hands before."

"I'll chip in for half the buy-in. It'll be fun!" Stella's eyes lit up, her aura tinged with flashes of orange and pink—colours that screamed enthusiasm.

Khynzy smiled back, her gaze lingering on Stella for a moment longer than usual. Despite Stella's bubbly demeanour and seemingly carefree spirit, Khynzy knew about her burdens. Stella had come from a family that had once financially struggled, a past that had shaped her resilience and resourcefulness. She'd been instrumental in helping her parents revive their small business, even if it meant that her savings took a hit. It wasn't something Stella talked about often, but her actions—like offering to split the buy-in—spoke volumes about her character.

"It's kind of you to offer," Khynzy said softly. "But are you sure you're okay with sharing the buy-in?" Khynzy asked cautiously. "It's quite a lot, and you've been doing much for your family lately. There's no guarantee you'll get it back."

Stella's aura morphed, the colours deepening into shades of lavender and teal—markers of wisdom and loyalty. "Things are slowly getting better for us, you know. Besides, what are friends for if we can't share a little risk and a lot of fun?"

"Alright," Khynzy agreed, laying out the terms. "You're on. If I win, you get your buy-in back first. After that, half of the remaining winnings will go to charity, a quarter into my savings, and we'll share the last quarter for some fun. How does that sound?"

Stella grinned. "Perfect! Deal." She then made a small fist-pumping gesture and exclaimed, "Fighting!"

Khynzy chuckled, "You and your K-Drama expressions. Alright, see you tomorrow night, Stella."

As Stella walked away, Khynzy couldn't help but think how lucky she was to have a friend like her. Stella was a bright, colourful tapestry of positive energies in a world where auras revealed the unseen and often unspoken layers of human emotion. And even though she had her own set of challenges, her light shone undiminished—a constant reminder that adversity could be overcome with the right blend of optimism and action.

With that thought, Khynzy returned to her coding, her fingers dancing across the keyboard. The weekend lay ahead, promising not just a game of poker but another chapter in the unfolding story of friendships as complex and colourful as the auras she alone could see.

❦

As they entered the opulent casino the next day, the

atmosphere was charged with anticipation. The clinking of chips and the shuffling of cards filled the air, creating a sensory overload for Khynzy. The vibrant lights and the murmur of conversations further heightened her unease.

Khynzy had honed her ability to see auras over the years, and she knew that each player's aura could reveal more than their poker face ever could. She saw various colours and patterns swirling around each person, representing their emotions and intentions.

The first hand was dealt, and Khynzy observed the players. When it was her turn, she placed her bet while keeping an eye on the auras of her opponents. As the rounds continued, she noticed subtle shifts in their auras whenever they held strong hands or were just bluffing.

It wasn't long before Khynzy's intuition guided her to make strategic bets. She folded when she sensed the auras of her opponents revealing strong hands, and she confidently raised when she detected hesitation or anxiety. With each hand, she grew more attuned to the ebb and flow of the game, her gift allowing her to make decisions with uncanny accuracy.

Stella, initially sceptical, watched in amazement as Khynzy's stack of chips steadily grew. It was as if she had a sixth sense for the game, an ability to read the intentions of others in a way that transcended mere human perception.

As the hands were dealt, Khynzy continued to observe the intricate dance of auras that played out before her. Each player's aura seemed to pulsate with unique colours and patterns, revealing their inner thoughts and intentions.

The man to her left, Raver, had an aura that shifted between shades of green and yellow. His aura would burst into vibrant emerald hues when he held a strong hand, radiating confidence and certainty. Tonight, however, his aura remained a subdued yellow, betraying his uncertainty and fear as he held a weak hand.

Across from Raver, Sophia's aura was a shimmering mixture of blue and purple, with tendrils of silver threading through it. When she bluffed, her aura exhibited an enchanting display of indigo and lavender, concealing her true intentions behind an intricate tapestry of deceit. Khynzy noted the subtle flicker of silver threads in her aura, signalling her attempt to deceive the table while holding a weak hand—a pair of fours and a five.

The man to her right, Samuel, exuded a deep crimson aura when he bluffed, a bold display of bravado meant to intimidate his opponents. Tonight, his aura remained a muted pink, a telltale sign that he was holding a pair of sevens and struggling to maintain his composure.

Hours passed, and Khynzy's winnings continued to mount. Her plan to support charitable organisations was becoming a reality. She had managed to turn the unpredictable world of poker into a game of calculated intuition and skill.

10

The Casino Encounter

Amidst the casino's dimly lit interior, the poker tables buzzed with excitement as the lady player at Table 7 continued her winning streak. The news had spread like wildfire, drawing curious spectators from all corners of the casino floor.

The neon lights of the casino painted the night with a vibrant glow as Levi's eyes widened in astonishment. His heart quickened as he observed Khynzy, his colleague, seated at a poker table. It was a twist of fate he couldn't have anticipated—encountering her in such an unexpected setting.

Khynzy was a puzzle to Levi. With his gift of hearing negative or malicious thoughts from others, he rarely encountered anyone who piqued his curiosity as much as her. In this bustling casino, amidst the clatter of chips and the murmur of conversations, he hears nothing from her. She was a blank slate, an anomaly to his extraordinary ability. She remained his enigma, his sole exception. He couldn't help but wonder if she possessed a power akin to his own—a power to influence the game through unseen forces.

Stella, their vivacious colleague who had a penchant for involving Khynzy in her escapades, flashed a mischievous grin at Levi. "Caught you off guard, huh, new guy? Didn't expect to see someone familiar amidst all this temptation, did you?"

Levi cleared his throat, struggling to regain his composure. "No, it's just... surprising. I didn't think I'd run into anyone I knew here."

With a mischievous glint in her eye, Stella nudged him playfully. "Well, there you have it! Let me introduce you to our card shark—Khynzy."

Levi's heart raced as Stella led him closer to the poker table, allowing him a discreet vantage point to observe the unfolding drama.

With each card that Khynzy skilfully played, Levi couldn't help but be captivated. Her movements were calculated, her demeanour composed, as if she had mastered the art of high-stakes gambling. And to his bewilderment, he still couldn't hear a single negative thought from her. No trace of deceit or malice reached his senses. Her mind remained elusive, her thoughts hidden from his grasp. It was both a source of intrigue and a reminder that there was a part of her he could never influence.

Time slipped away as the hands of poker came and went. Stella's muted cheers punctuated each triumph, and Levi couldn't help but feel a sense of pride for his colleague's prowess.

Unaware of Levi's presence, Khynzy continued her game. Levi's phone buzzed. It was a text from his best friend, who had just arrived at the casino.

"Hey, I've got to go," Levi said to Stella. "My friend just showed up. But it was really something, watching Khynzy play."

"Sure thing," Stella replied. "Have fun with your friend. And yeah, she's quite the card shark, right?"

Levi agreed. "Definitely. Catch you later, Stella."

11

Quarter of Deuces

Every time Khynzy won a hand, she tipped the dealer. Each time she did, she noticed the dealer's aura shift from a reserved blue to a warm, appreciative golden hue. It was a subtle but meaningful transformation that only she could perceive.

As Khynzy continued to play, her intuition guided her to make strategic bets and well-timed folds. The colours and shapes of the auras around her served as a roadmap, allowing her to navigate the treacherous waters of poker with unparalleled precision.

The poker table was ablaze with anticipation as the next round commenced. Khynzy had become somewhat of a legend at the casino, her uncanny ability to read auras transforming her into a formidable player. But this time, the cards dealt to her seemed unkind—a pair of twos, a modest hand by any standard.

Seated across from her was a player known as Alex, a seasoned poker veteran with a reputation for his mastery of the game. He held an Ace and a King, a powerful starting hand that promised strength and control. His aura shimmered with confidence, a fiery blend of red and orange that seemed to match the fiery intensity of his play.

As the round progressed, Khynzy watched the auras of her fellow players, searching for the subtle shifts that would guide her decisions. The community cards were revealed one by one, and the tension in the room grew palpable.

The first three cards unveiled an Ace, a King, and a Two, giving Khynzy three twos and Alex a pair of Aces and Kings. Khynzy's aura, a soothing symphony of pastels, remained steady, while Alex's blazed with a fiery intensity, reflecting his growing confidence.

Khynzy now held three twos, a much stronger hand. But Alex's aura continued to radiate with fiery determination. The fourth card was unveiled, and it was an Ace, giving Alex three Aces and two Kings. Confident with his full house, Alex boldly pushed most of his chips into the centre of the table. The other players quickly folded, leaving Khynzy facing her intimidating opponent.

The room seemed to hold its breath as the final card was turned over.

It was another Two. Khynzy had achieved four of a kind—quad twos. Once calm and serene, her aura now sparkled with a soft, silvery brilliance, reflecting her inner triumph. But her facial expression remained the same.

Khynzy took a moment to assess her hand and the aura of those around her. She knew that she had an extraordinary hand, but there was a possibility that Alex might have a better four-of-a-kind — four Aces. But she sensed something within Alex's aura—an undercurrent of desperation that he was hiding behind his fiery exterior. This insight convinced Khynzy that Alex's best possible hand was a full house.

With a calm, collected demeanour, she matched Alex's bet and then raised it, her aura shining even more brilliantly. Alex hesitated, his aura flickering with uncertainty for the first time. He eventually called her raise, and they revealed their hands.

Khynzy calmly displayed her quad twos while Alex's confident aura faltered as he revealed his full house. The room erupted into cheers and applause as Khynzy's aura sparkled with the sweet taste of victory.

She had turned a seemingly weak hand into an extraordinary triumph, all thanks to her unique ability to read auras. Her gift had allowed her to navigate the unpredictable world of poker with skill and intuition, turning the odds in her favour when it seemed impossible.

As the night came to an end, Khynzy was declared the winner. "Congratulations!" Stella exclaimed, her eyes wide in disbelief. "You're like a poker prodigy!"

Khynzy grinned, feeling the satisfaction of the win and the pleasure of the secret she harboured. She could see the auras surrounding each player, giving her an uncanny insight into their intentions and emotions—a gift she had never disclosed, even to Stella.

Standing at a distance with his friend Owen, Levi watched as Khynzy and Stella celebrated.

Owen noticed Levi's gaze fixed on Khynzy.

"Who's that?" Owen asked.

"That's Khynzy. She just won big time at poker," Levi said, still entranced.

Owen grinned. "Really? First time I've seen you this captivated. You know her personally?"

Levi smirked. "She's a colleague—same company, different squads. Maybe she's my type."

Owen chuckled and nudged Levi. "Well, well, looks like someone caught your eye for once."

With that, they both left the casino, Levi still puzzled by how Khynzy managed to win so decisively, completely unaware of any special abilities she might possess.

12

Codes and Cards

In the meeting area, a quiet corner tucked away from the main office space, just the two of them, Levi and Khynzy, found themselves discussing a project that had captured their attention. Charts and diagrams adorned the whiteboard, and as they exchanged ideas, a sense of mutual respect and admiration grew between them.

Levi leaned against the table, his arms crossed, as he listened to Khynzy's suggestions. Her words were thoughtful, each idea backed by a clear understanding of the software's intricacies. He marvelled at how her mind worked, the precision with which she dissected complex problems and proposed elegant solutions.

As Khynzy spoke, Levi couldn't help but admire her intellect. He noticed the way her eyes sparkled with passion, the determination that radiated from her every word. Her insights were invaluable, and he found himself genuinely excited to see how their collaboration would unfold.

"I think your idea could streamline the user interface," Levi interjected, adding his thoughts to the conversation. "And we could implement that data validation technique you mentioned to improve data accuracy."

Khynzy's eyes lit up with appreciation, a smile tugging at the corners of her lips. "Exactly," she agreed, her presence radiating with a vibrant energy. "It's like you're reading my mind."

Levi chuckled, a playful glint in his eyes. Little did Khynzy know that his abilities often allowed him to do just that. But with her, it was different. There was a comfortable camaraderie between them, a connection beyond his ability to hear thoughts.

As the meeting progressed, Levi immersed himself in the flow of ideas, his thoughts intertwining seamlessly with Khynzy's. It was a rare experience for him, one that he cherished. He was amazed at how their skills and insights complemented each other.

Yet, amidst their discussion, a stray thought slipped into Levi's mind, almost as if it had a life of its own. He found himself realising the subtle details about Khynzy's appearance–the elegance in the simplicity of her style, the absence of heavy makeup, her almond-shaped eyes, slim nose, and the shape of her lips - not too thin or thick, but just right. And he couldn't help but be drawn to her small, pretty, heart-shaped face. What was he thinking? He shook his head inwardly, urging himself to focus on what she was saying.

Meanwhile, Khynzy noticed that Levi's presence had a certain allure. She could catch whiffs of his subtle yet captivating perfume, and his neat attire exuded a sense of professionalism and confidence. Standing almost a head taller than her, he carried himself with an air of quiet authority that she found intriguing.

She had to admit that she appreciated how he engaged with her, respecting her ideas and genuinely listening to her suggestions. Despite the faint distraction from his pleasing scent and presence, she tried to focus on the task.

But Khynzy couldn't help but notice how Levi's blue eyes

sparkled as they conversed. His passion for his work and keen intellect were evident in every word he spoke. She admired his ability to easily navigate complex challenges and his creativity in finding innovative solutions.

After the meeting concluded, they lingered in the meeting area, their conversation shifting to more personal topics. The office noise faded into the background as they talked about their interests and hobbies and even shared a few anecdotes from their lives outside of work.

Suddenly, Levi's thoughts drifted to a previous night. He had spotted Khynzy at the casino, winning big time at poker. The memory brought a smile to his face. "You know, I saw you at the casino the other night," he began, his tone casual.

Khynzy looked surprised for a moment before breaking into a grin. "Oh, you caught me," she replied, her eyes twinkling with amusement. "Yes, I was trying my luck at poker."

Levi raised an eyebrow, intrigued. "And it seems luck was definitely on your side."

Khynzy shrugged modestly. "I guess so. I managed to pull off some good hands."

Levi leaned in, his curiosity growing. "I have to admit, I was quite impressed by your poker skills."

Khynzy laughed. "Well, don't be too impressed. It was mostly just a fun night out."

Levi smiled, enjoying the easy banter between them. "Fun night out or not, you certainly made an impression. Winning big at poker is no small feat."

Khynzy's cheeks tinged with a hint of pink, and she looked away momentarily. "Thank you," she murmured, her voice soft.

Levi couldn't help but admire her even more. Not only was she brilliant in software development, but she also had a flair for poker. It was an unexpected combination that added to her charm.

Their connection was undeniable, a meeting of minds with the promise of collaboration and understanding. As they eventually parted ways to resume their tasks, a sense of anticipation lingered in the air.

13

An Unexpected Invitation

Amidst the hustle and bustle of the office, Rachel's presence stood out to Levi, though not for reasons he'd readily admit. Rachel, a business analyst in his squad, seemed eager to spend more time with him. While he valued their professional relationship, he was less enthusiastic about anything more than that.

One afternoon, as Levi focused on his work, Rachel appeared beside him. Her bleached blonde hair cascaded in loose waves around her face, and her hazel eyes held a playful twinkle.

"Hey, Levi," she started, her voice imbued with an unmistakable enthusiasm. "I'm planning a poker night this weekend at my place. Would you like to come?"

Levi stopped typing and looked up, meeting her gaze. "Poker night, you say? Sounds fun."

"It will be," Rachel assured, her eyes lighting up. "It's a low-key affair—just a few of us from the team. A good chance to hang out outside of work."

Levi hesitated. As he did, his unusual gift activated; he heard Rachel's thoughts as if she'd spoken them aloud. She was hoping for more than just friendly camaraderie. She wanted him to let his guard down, maybe have a few drinks, and become more... available.

"I'll think about it and let you know," Levi responded, choosing his words carefully to sidestep the implied invitation in her thoughts.

Rachel's smile wavered slightly, but she nodded. "Sure, no pressure."

Levi sat back, contemplating. If more people were invited and he stayed sober, he could likely sidestep any designs Rachel might have.

And then it struck him—why not bring Khynzy's team into the mix? The thought of socialising with her in a non-work setting was appealing. This could be his chance to connect with her on a different level, away from the stress and formalities of the workplace.

He weighed the pros and cons, turning the idea over in his mind. As the hours passed, his decision solidified. This was an opportunity he couldn't miss, a strategic move that could benefit him professionally and personally.

After carefully composing his thoughts, Levi typed a message to Rachel: "I've thought it over, and I'm in for poker night. How about we also extend the invitation to the Code squad? It could foster good relations between our squads."

He hit send and then quickly typed another message. "By the way, I hope it's cool that I extended the invitation. I just wanted to ensure we're on the same page—I'm only looking for a friendly hangout."

Rachel's reply came within minutes, her words bursting with enthusiasm. "Sounds like a plan! And no worries, it's all good. I'll send out the invites."

Levi leaned back in his chair, satisfied. If all went well, this could be the opening he'd been waiting for, the first step toward deeper conversations and closer connections. And as he imagined a relaxed evening of poker, laughter, and casual chats with Khynzy, a grin began to form at the edges of his lips. Undoubtedly, It was a risk, but one he was willing to take.

Meanwhile, in Rachel's mind, a different script was playing out. Her thoughts resonated with a fervent desire to spend quality time with Levi. The invitation was her way of drawing him closer, hoping that an intimate setting might unveil the feelings she'd harboured for him. *Maybe next time it could just be the two of us,* she mused, an almost obsessive yearning in her thoughts. She couldn't help but wonder if Levi had a thing for Khynzy. After all, Khynzy was a part of the Code squad, which may be why Levi wanted to invite them, too. What is it in Khynzy that he likes? These thoughts swirled in her mind as she set about sending the invitations.

As the invitation reached Khynzy's team, a ripple of excitement spread. The idea of a combined poker night sounded intriguing, an opportunity to bridge the gap between their departments and foster collaboration. For Khynzy, the prospect of seeing Levi in a more relaxed setting brought a flutter of nerves, along with a hint of excitement she couldn't entirely suppress.

14

Unspoken Strategies

"Levi, welcome! Glad you could make it." Rachel's voice carried a veneer of warmth as she greeted him. Her eyes flickered between Levi and Khynzy, noting their proximity with curiosity and a tinge of frustration she hoped he couldn't detect.

Each arrived at Rachel's apartment simultaneously, drawn by a mutual interest in poker and an unspoken curiosity about the other's skills. Khynzy took her seat at the table, and Levi naturally gravitated to the spot next to her. "Mind if I sit beside you?" he asked calmly, a subtle smile gracing his lips. His choice of seat wasn't just about strategy; it was also about forging a connection beyond words.

Hoping to spend more time with Levi, Rachel had strategically arranged the poker night. Her aura pulsed with excitement and impatience, revealing her true intentions to anyone who could see. She secretly hoped Levi would choose the seat next to her, a desire that her aura had broadcasted.

However, the universe had a different plan. Levi settled beside Khynzy, a decision that Rachel struggled to mask her disappointment over. Her thoughts brimmed with annoyance and envy, in stark contrast to the composed smile she wore.

Rachel's aura speaks volumes about her unspoken feelings for Levi. Khynzy wished she could do the same to Levi—read his aura and discern whether he felt the same way. But his aura remained hidden, a mystery she couldn't unravel.

"Feeling lucky tonight?" Khynzy's question directed at Levi was met with a chuckle. "Luck has its moments, but tonight, it's about strategy." His reply carried a note of mystery, hinting at the secrets he held within his mind.

The room's atmosphere became thick with concentration; every player was engrossed in the rhythmic dance of the game: the shuffle of cards, the clinking of chips, and the subtle tell given away by fleeting expressions. Amidst the players, two figures stood out: Levi and Khynzy.

With his astute gaze, Levi had an uncanny talent for tapping into the negative thoughts of those around him. This ability granted him an edge, an intimate knowledge of their uncertainties, regrets, and fears.

During a key round, Levi honed in on the thoughts buzzing around the table. A thread of insecurity whispered from Max, *This hand is trash. I've overplayed my previous one.* From Kevin, doubt gnawed sharply, *Levi might have that straight. I always corner myself.* Using this knowledge, Levi adjusted his strategy, pushing Max further into doubt and bluffing Kevin into a premature fold.

Yet, with Khynzy, he was met with silence—a void he could neither penetrate nor understand. He shot her a glance, the words slipping out with a mix of challenge and amusement, "Always full of surprises, aren't you?"

Khynzy, with her ability to perceive the auras of those around her, had always prided herself on her unerring intuition. Each player emitted colours that betrayed their true emotions and intentions. But Levi? There was only an impenetrable void. No colours, no hints; it felt like chasing shadows in the dark.

Meeting Levi's challenging gaze, her lips curved into a knowing smile. "It wouldn't be fun if it was easy, would it?" she replied, her voice tinged with playful defiance.

Everyone's eyes were on Levi and Khynzy as the night went on. Their back-and-fourths added spice to the room. The others, caught up in their intense showdown, became more like audience members, hooked on every move between them. Throughout the night, it was like the two were in their own world, battling it out. They had their unique ways, making the game look like a mix of mind games and strategy. Every play felt like there was more to it than met the eye.

In the end, both Levi and Khynzy came out on top. Their wins weren't just about being good players but reading the game and each other perfectly.

❦

After the poker game, everyone transitioned to Rachel's living room for charades. Stella had suggested the change of game, and the idea was welcomed.

Team One: Levi, Paul, Abby, Rachel, and Kevin

Team Two: Khynzy, Stella, Jennie, Tim, and Max

Jennie was the first to pick a folded paper, which read, 'Internet Slang: Carpe diem–Seize the Day.' She mimed grabbing something out of the air. Although dressed casually, she looked visibly anxious. Her internal voice murmured, *Carpe diem, they better get this.* Paul guessed, "Taking Charge," but Levi, sensing her anxious thoughts, confidently corrected with "Carpe diem."

Stella's turn was next. Her slip read, 'Internet Slang: SMH–Shaking My Head.' She acted like she was swiping left on a smartphone, then shook her head in disappointment. Khynzy, sensing the frustration in her aura, guessed, "SMH."

In a cosy sweater, Abby reached for her paper, which stated, 'Internet Slang: TIL–Today I Learned.' She acted like she was reading a book and pretended a light bulb went above her head. Her thoughts swirled with anxiety. *Come on,* *it's TIL. They have to get it.** Levi heard her anxious thoughts and immediately guessed, "TIL."

Rachel, attempting to capture Khynzy's usual office style, donned a meticulously selected preppy outfit. Choosing her slip next, it read, 'Emoji: Heart Eyes.' With exaggerated emphasis, she formed heart shapes over her eyes, her gaze steadfast on Levi. Her thoughts were singular; Levi must discern that these Heart Eyes are solely for him. "So, head over heels for Levi, are we?" Jennie teased, sparking a wave of laughter throughout the room.

Despite the surrounding jovial chaos, Khynzy, attired in a blend of casual and subtly preppy clothes suitable for the informal gathering, perceived Rachel's veiled obsession. The overt heart-eye gesture made her conclusion straightforward. "Heart Eyes," she stated correctly. A fleeting wonder crossed her mind about Rachel's abrupt alteration in style, sensing an imitation of her sartorial choice.

Paul, dressed in jeans and a button-up, picked his paper. It read, 'Internet Slang: FOMO–Fear Of Missing Out.' He acted out snoring, then waking up in a panic. His thoughts were fearful;* *They must get that it's FOMO. Please.** Levi picked up on the fear and guessed, "FOMO."

Tim's turn came up, wearing his sports jersey. His paper read, 'Internet Slang: YOLO–You Only Live Once.' He made a motion of tying a rope to his ankles and then pretended to leap, bouncing back up with imaginary elasticity. Internally, he fretted, *If they don't guess YOLO, I'll look foolish.** Max tried with, "Jumping off a cliff?" and Stella ventured, "Taking a leap of faith?" but it was Levi, tapping into Tim's apprehensive thoughts, who accurately guessed, "YOLO."

Kevin, dressed in business casual attire, took his turn. His slip read, 'Internet Slang: Mic Drop.' With confidence, he pantomimed holding a microphone and then dramatically dropped it. Levi instantly knew it represented 'Mic Drop', but

Tim beat him to it before he could say anything, announcing, "Mic Drop."

Khynzy's paper was next, and it read, 'Emoji: Tears Of Joy.' She acted like she was laughing so hard she was crying.

Levi watched Khynzy act out her emoji with inexplicable fascination. There was something refreshingly genuine about her laughter and exaggerated expressions that he couldn't put his finger on.

Paul guessed, "You're laughing, LOL?" and Abby offered, "Joking?" Finally, Levi guessed right: "Tears Of Joy." Khynzy felt a strange warmth wash over her as she locked eyes with Levi. She couldn't decipher why his smile made her feel so happy, but it did.

Finally, it was Levi's turn. Levi felt his heart rate accelerate as he unfolded the small slip of paper. 'Emoji: Kiss- Woman, Man.' A flash of hesitation crossed his mind, the thought of quietly placing the slip back fleeting, but he brushed it away. Taking a deep breath, he stepped into the centre of the room.

First, he tapped his chest to signify "man." His teammates nodded.

"Okay, it's about a guy or a man," Kevin announced, adding a touch of levity to the focused room.

Levi then pointed directly at Khynzy. The room's attention instantly pivoted toward her. She looked up, visibly surprised but intrigued.

As Khynzy looked around the room, she noticed a sudden change in Rachel's aura. It shifted to a colour of envy, perhaps even bordering on jealousy or anger.

"Ooh, spicy! Love is in the air," Jennie commented, eliciting laughter and whispers.

Before Levi could make his final gesture, Stella's voice piped up from behind, "You're in love with Khynzy!"

Laughter and hoots erupted, but Levi stayed focused. He brought his index finger to his lips and then gestured toward

Khynzy's lips.

After a moment of silence, someone finally yelled, "It's the 'Kiss: Woman, Man' emoji!"

"Correct," Levi confirmed, returning to his seat amid playful ribbing and nudges from his team.

Khynzy felt her cheeks warm up, a blush spreading across her face. The moment—tinged with humour, a wrong guess, and a hint of something more—had added an unexpected layer to their casual acquaintance, making both wonder what the next round might hold.

As the game progressed, it became clear that Levi and Khynzy had a particular knack for guessing—thanks to their unique but undisclosed abilities. And as the final round of charades came to a close, laughter filled the room, a testament to newfound camaraderie.

15

The Panda Drumm3r

Levi's Sunday evening took an unexpected twist when doing a casual scroll through his social media feed. His fingertips halted as a mesmerising drumbeat tapped its way into his ears. Intrigued, his eyes focused on a live stream where the beats constructed an invisible allure.

Hidden behind a playful paper bag mask decorated with panda eyes, the drummer radiated an enchanting allure, marrying her enigmatic persona with masterful playing. Beneath her slightly sheer, long-sleeved black mesh shirt peeked a sweetheart tube top, elegantly accentuating her curves and conjuring a sophisticated image amid rhythmic fervour. Torn skinny black jeans subtly showcased her shapely legs, infusing a rebellious allure. White sneakers, unpretentious and ordinary, adeptly engaged the pedals beneath, mainly through a side-angle camera that adeptly highlighted her effortless bass pedal work.

Her hands were manipulating the drumsticks with ease, making the drumming appear incredibly cool and almost second nature. There was an undeniable finesse in how her wrists flicked, sending the sticks crisply against the snare, and a subtle strength displayed as they rebounded seamlessly from the toms. The sticks danced, twirled, and struck with precision, turning the act of drumming into a visually compelling art form.

Her slender and statuesque silhouette hinted at a life or profession far removed from the hidden musician who now commanded the stage. With a brown bag shrouding her identity, each precise drumstick motion became a subtle proclamation of expertise, devoid of self-display. Levi was irresistibly drawn in, ensnared by a rhythmic domain where mystery and mastery crafted a uniquely beguiling performance.

The view count soared, and a cascade of comments flooded the screen—praise, awe, and exclamations of delight. Amidst the many reactions, a username stood out: "PandaDrumm3r." It was the moniker of the mysterious lady drummer who had captured everyone's attention. The chat section buzzed with emoticons, comments, and words of astonishment.

"Go, Panda Drumm3r!"

"Who is she? Her talent is off the charts!"

The comment section illuminated with positivity, a collective admiration binding the online community together in shared awe of the mysterious performer's artistry. Fans theorised about the persona beneath the bag, while others simply lost themselves in the rich tapestry of beats she expertly wove.

However, a jarring word — 'butterface', abruptly surfaced amidst the sea of positivity, sowing a seed of discord among the unity. For a moment, the stream's harmony was tainted by the disrespectful slang, which, embedded in the casual cruelty of internet language, implied an appreciation for a woman's body while demeaning her facial appearance – 'but her face.'

Levi's brow furrowed at the sudden injection of negativity, incongruent amidst the sea of appreciation and admiration.

Immediately, a wave of defenders rose from the digital audience, condemning the unkind remark and reinforcing the atmosphere of admiration that had initially defined the virtual space.

"What does looks have to do with her skill?"

"I bet she's adorable, just like a panda!"

"Who cares about looks when you can play like that?!"

Levi, moved by the communal defence and the unyielding skill of the hidden drummer, joined the fortress of supportive voices, adding, "Perhaps her true beauty is in the unseen, where we are left to appreciate the soulful beats undistracted. Her artistry is a pure gift that needs no face to be appreciated."

Levi continued to watch, drawn to the music like a moth to a flame. He was not just captivated by the rhythm but also by the aura surrounding the performance. An undeniable sense of power and artistry was woven into each stroke of the drumsticks.

As the video concluded, Levi hesitated for a moment before clicking on the profile link. He was directed to a channel that promised more—a collection of drum covers that reverberated with passion and skill. Each video maintained the same camera angle, solely focused on the drums and the distinctive paper bag-clad head. The anonymity of the drummer intrigued him, adding an air of mystique to the already enchanting music. Without a second thought, Levi pressed the 'Follow' button.

He found himself nestled within a novel emotion, a surprising yet gentle realisation that he might just have developed a celebrity crush on the masked drummer. Her seductive talent, the mysterious allure, and that raw, rhythmic energy that had seeped through the digital waves had kindled a flame of admiration and curiosity within him, leaving him to marvel in the afterglow of her resonant performance.

16

Levi's Peculiar Interest

The next day, as the meeting about the new software app continued, Levi couldn't help but find himself amused and intrigued by Khynzy's sleep-deprived appearance. Her dark circles and the evident struggle to stay awake amused him in a way he hadn't expected.

In the past, Levi had effortlessly manipulated the thoughts of countless individuals, but Khynzy proved to be an enigma. His previous attempts to infiltrate her mind had been met with unexpected resistance. He found himself captivated by this challenge, a challenge that transcended the ordinary mental manipulations he was accustomed to.

His fascination extended beyond the work environment. He had tried to connect with her during group activities like poker and charades at a colleague's house, but it wasn't enough. He longed for a deeper, more personal interaction, a one-on-one where he could truly delve into her essence without the interference of others.

Seeing her fight to keep her eyes open, an idea emerged—perhaps a relaxed private dinner would pave the way for a closer connection.

As their meeting crossed the halfway mark and a 15-

minute break was announced, most of their colleagues seized the opportunity to stretch their legs, heading towards the office kitchen to refill their coffee mugs, leaving them in a comfortable bubble. Levi decided to take a chance. He leaned forward in his chair, cleared his throat, and addressed Khynzy, his tone casual and friendly.

"Hey," he began, "I couldn't help but notice you look like you could use a break from work. What do you think about grabbing dinner tonight? Just thought it might be nice to unwind a bit, and I could use some company. Could be fun."

Khynzy, caught off guard by the unexpected invitation, blinked in surprise, pulling herself out of her project-laden thoughts to process his words.

"And hey, zero pressure. Totally understand if you'd rather head home and rest." He added, his smile light and understanding.

Stella, who'd stayed behind, nudged Khynzy gently with a mischievous yet gentle grin. "Go on, Khynzy," she whispered. "You could use a break."

Khynzy hesitated for a moment, her thoughts racing. Without being able to see Levi's aura, discerning his true intentions was a challenge. Nonetheless, she felt an undeniable attraction to him, a pull of curiosity that she found herself eager to explore.

Finally, she nodded, her exhaustion evident in her voice. "Sure, that sounds nice. Dinner tonight would be great."

A glimmer of satisfaction flashed in Levi's eyes as he realised his plan had worked. Appreciative of her company for the casual dinner ahead, an opportunity to get closer to her and perhaps uncover the mysteries that made her resist his mental influence. As the meeting continued, Levi couldn't help but wonder what lay ahead.

At 6 p.m., Levi found himself in an unfamiliar and somewhat uncomfortable position. For the first time in a long while, he felt nervous about dinner. As he approached Khynzy's desk to pick her up, his heart quickened its pace, and he couldn't shake the sense of anticipation that tingled in the air.

Khynzy looked up from her work, her tired eyes brightening as she saw Levi. She offered him a warm smile, appreciative of the break from her demanding schedule. "Hi, Levi," she greeted him.

"Hello, Khynzy," he replied, his voice a touch more uncertain than he had intended. He cleared his throat. "Are you ready?"

Khynzy gathered her belongings and rose from her desk, joining Levi as they made their way to the exit. It was a quiet journey to the car, the tension between them palpable. Levi couldn't help but steal glances at her, his mind racing with questions about this intriguing woman who had captured his attention.

He had chosen a fancy restaurant for their dinner. It was a place known for its exquisite cuisine and elegant ambience. Levi hoped the setting would help ease his nervousness and create an atmosphere conducive to meaningful conversation.

As they entered the restaurant and were seated at a table bathed in soft candlelight, Khynzy couldn't help but feel a sense of awe. The place was one of the new restaurants she wanted to try.

"Levi, this place is incredible," she remarked, her eyes sparkling excitedly.

He smiled, relieved that his choice had met with her approval. "I'm glad you like it, Khynzy. I thought it would be a nice change of pace."

Their dinner progressed, and Levi kept the conversation light and engaging. He asked her about her work and her thoughts on various topics. Khynzy responded with genuine enthusiasm, slowly letting her guard down in his company.

As the evening wore on, Levi couldn't ignore the growing curiosity about Khynzy's sleepless nights and her persistent exhaustion. Khynzy noticed a gentle concern in Levi's gaze, a flicker of something that made her pause mid-sentence. He leaned slightly forward, his voice soft and filled with sincerity. "Khynzy, I couldn't help but notice you seem quite tired. Is there something bothering you? Do you have trouble sleeping?"

Her heart skipped a beat at his perceptiveness, a warmth blooming in her chest at his genuine concern. She offered a grateful smile, touched by his question. "I appreciate you noticing, Levi. It's just that I've been practising a hobby quite a bit."

Levi's eyes held a mixture of curiosity and interest. "Oh? A hobby? I've been meaning to ask what you enjoy doing in your free time."

Khynzy felt her cheeks flush slightly, a combination of bashfulness and excitement bubbling within her. She took a sip of her drink before replying. "Well, I play the drums. It's something I've loved for a long time, and it's a way for me to unwind."

Levi's gaze sparkled with intrigue. "You play the drums? That's incredible, Khynzy! I had no idea. Do you play in a band or just for fun?"

She hesitated for a moment before sharing, "Well, I create drum covers of songs I like. I upload them online. It's just a fun way for me to express myself."

Levi was intrigued. "That sounds interesting. What platform do you use to share your drum covers?"

Khynzy's cheeks flushed slightly as she admitted, "I have an account on several social platforms. I've never shown my face in any of my videos, though. I wear a brown bag over my head to hide my identity."

Levi's eyes widened in surprise. "Wait a minute... are you

the lady drummer I follow? The one who's always wearing a brown bag with panda eyes?"

Khynzy couldn't help but laugh. "Guilty as charged. That's me."

A genuine admiration lit Levi's face. "I love your drum covers! I had no idea it was you. Your talent is incredible."

She tilted her head, allowing a gracious "Thanks" to slip out before her eyes twinkled with playful curiosity. "How about you? Do you play any instruments?"

His eyes lit up, and a warm smile unfolded across his face. "Yes, I do. I play the guitar, particularly rock songs. There's something about the energy in rock music that I love."

Khynzy nodded, a wistful smile tugging at her lips. "Absolutely. The vibrancy and authenticity in rock music are unparalleled. But it seems like rock bands are becoming a rare breed with the surge of electronic music everywhere."

Levi sighed, leaning back, "You're spot on. Electronic music has its own vibe and audience, but it feels like it has overshadowed the rawness and authenticity that comes with rock. There was something intrinsically real about a group of people creating music together, each instrument, each voice, adding a unique flavour."

Their conversation flowed effortlessly, their connection deepening with every shared story and revelation. As the night came to an end, Levi offered to drive Khynzy home.

During the car ride, Levi's fingers twitched on the steering wheel, the rhythm of an unplayed beat pulsating through his veins as he navigated the city streets. His mind was engulfed in waves of astonishment. He had always been interested in Khynzy; apart from being strikingly his type in the looks department and a brilliantly skilled software developer, she was also uniquely immune to his ability to discern negative thoughts. Now, the enigmatic drummer, concealed behind a playful panda-eyed brown bag in those viral videos—the one he had a celebrity crush on—was sitting beside him and was, astonishingly, the same person. How was this even possible?

He couldn't help but smile. "You know, since we're both into music, maybe we could jam together sometime."

Khynzy's eyes lit up at the suggestion. "I'd love that! We should definitely plan a jam session."

With that, they arrived at her doorstep, their shared passions and newfound connection promising the possibility of beautiful harmonies and rhythms yet to be unveiled.

17

Duet of Preparations

As the workweek wrapped up on Friday, both Levi and Khynzy, though parting ways, hurried home with a shared sense of excitement. They had agreed to a jamming session at Khynzy's place the next day, a plan that set their hearts racing with anticipation.

Khynzy's apartment became a flurry of activity as she prepared for Levi's visit. She meticulously vacuumed each room, ensuring no corner was left untouched. Her focus then shifted to her sacred space – the music room. There, her drum set stood proudly, each drum polished to a shine, the cymbals gleaming under the room's light. She adjusted the stands, aligned her drumsticks, and fine-tuned the equipment. It was more than just cleaning; it was a ritual, a way of setting the stage for the creative synergy she anticipated.

The dilemma of choosing the right outfit was next. Standing in front of her closet, Khynzy eyed her array of clothes. Her usual live-stream outfits, particularly her favourite – a black mesh long-sleeved top with a sweetheart tube underneath paired with ripped black skinny jeans, were stylish and flattering, designed to accentuate her curves in a tasteful way. But this occasion called for something different;

it was a casual, personal setting, not a performance. She wanted her outfit to reflect that – to be comfortable and suitable for an intimate jamming session while still maintaining a sense of her personal style.

First, she considered a rock band shirt paired with straight-cut jeans, a nod to the musical theme of the day. But this combo felt too plain, too akin to just 'one of the guys.' She wanted to strike a balance – something that was true to her style but also fitting for the casual nature of their meeting.

After some thought, she narrowed it down to two options. Her first choice was a pair of ripped denim shorts combined with a casual white tank top. This look was effortlessly cool and comfortable, exuding a relaxed and approachable vibe while subtly highlighting her figure. It was a familiar style that made her feel confident and at ease.

The second option was a more playful and stylish ensemble: a pair of skorts that offered both comfort and flair, paired with a fitted 3/4 sleeved white shirt. This outfit was a blend of playful charm and sophistication, showcasing her well-toned legs and complementing her curves in a manner that was tasteful and chic.

Both outfits lay on her bed, each a contender for the next day's session. She decided she would choose in the morning, depending on the mood that greeted her.

With the options set, Khynzy turned her attention to winding down for the night. She cleaned up the clutter, took a long, soothing bath, and finally, before slipping into bed, she carefully placed an eye patch over her eyes. 'Panda eyes' – the term she amusingly used for dark circles – were not welcome tomorrow. She needed to be fresh, vibrant, and at her best, both musically and in appearance, for what she hoped would be a memorable day of rhythm and connection.

Levi, on the other hand, found himself chuckling at his own reflection in the mirror. It was just a casual jamming session, yet there he was, fussing over outfits as if it were a date. He settled on a grey shirt and jeans, ironing them meticulously and even laying out matching socks and shoes for the next day.

His next task was a rehearsal. Picking up his guitar, Levi began to run through a playlist of songs, ones he thought would complement Khynzy's drumming. It wasn't just about brushing up his guitar skills but about creating a harmonious blend with her rhythm. He practised diligently, his fingers strumming and picking, ensuring each note would mesh perfectly with the beat of her drums. As he played, he imagined their session – the blend of guitar and drums filling the room, a testament to their shared passion for music.

He lost himself in the practice, occasionally pausing to scribble down a song that struck him as a perfect fit for their collaboration. Levi wanted to impress Khynzy, not just with his playing but with his understanding of their musical synergy. After hours of practice, he gently placed his guitar back in its case, his mind resonating with tunes and eager anticipation for the rhythmic dance they would share the next day.

18

The Rhythm of Attraction

Khynzy was engrossed in tweaking the pitch on her drum kit in her soundproof room. She had left the door slightly ajar to hear when Levi arrived. Just as she was tightening the last drumhead, the distinct chime of her doorbell filled the apartment. She inhaled deeply to calm her racing heart and darted to answer it.

As she swung the door open, there he was—Levi, standing casually in a grey crew-neck shirt and distressed jeans, holding a guitar case. Though his outfit was simple, he looked irresistibly good. The scent of his signature cologne enveloped her senses, making her feel dizzy in the best way possible.

"You look amazing," Levi grinned, taking in Khynzy's notably different outfit from her livestream get-ups - a casual tank top and denim shorts, in contrast to her usual black mesh with a tube top beneath. Somehow, he found this simpler attire, absent of her typical streaming glamour, uniquely sexy and attractive. "There's something about you in laid-back attire that's just...wow."

Khynzy felt her cheeks turn a shade pinker. "You're not so bad yourself," she retorted, stepping aside to let him in.

"Where do you want me to set this up?" Levi asked, pointing to his guitar case.

"Follow me," Khynzy led him to her sanctuary—her drum room.

"Whoa," he exclaimed as he stepped into the room. It was fully equipped, wall-to-wall, with soundproof foam and various music gadgets. "This is where the magic happens?"

"Among other things, yeah," she nodded, grinning from ear to ear. "Ready to jam?"

"Let's do this," he agreed, taking out his guitar and beginning to tune it.

While he was engrossed in the strings, Khynzy took a moment to watch him. His fingers danced gracefully over the fretboard, each movement deliberate and skilled. He looked up to catch her staring and shot her a playful smile.

"Like what you see?" he quipped.

Flustered, Khynzy giggled. "Well, you do know your way around a guitar."

He chuckled. "You're not too bad with those drumsticks yourself."

Levi's eyes fell on a sticker affixed to her drum kit, reading 'Panda Drumm3r'.

"I know it's your moniker, but I've never asked—how'd you land on 'Panda Drummer'?"

"The panda eyes aren't just cosmetic," she laughed, pointing to her eyes, which looked surprisingly bright today. "Sometimes, dark circles appear around my eyes when I struggle with sleep." Levi had seen her 'panda eyes' before—the dark circles from countless nights of less-than-adequate sleep. He found them strangely charming, an imperfect mark of her passion for her craft.

"Plus, I love pandas, and I love drumming. It just seemed to fit," Khynzy added.

"That's cool. It's fun and catchy…" Levi chuckled. His gaze

lingered on the '3' in 'Panda Drumm3r'. "I get the panda and drummer part," he added, a playful curiosity dancing in his eyes, "But what's with the '3'?"

Khynzy let out a small, amused sigh, "Ah, the mystery of the '3'. Well, when I first tried to create my online presence, 'Panda Drummer'—spelt the regular way—was already taken. So, I swapped out the 'e' for a '3'. A bit of digital creativity, if you will. It makes it unique, don't you think?"

"It does. Ever thought of giving me a cool name?" Levi teased.

"How about Wolf Strummer?" Khynzy suggested. "You have this sort of lone-wolf vibe, and the strumming part is pretty self-explanatory."

"I like it. Wolf Strummer it is," he agreed, clearly pleased.

For the next few hours, the room reverberated with the sounds of their synchronised playing. They jammed through several popular tracks. Although they considered live-streaming their playful musical explorations, the joy of the moment eclipsed any urgency to finalise plans, permitting them to simply bask in the mutual enjoyment of their impromptu ensemble.

"Ever get nervous before going live?" Levi asked during a brief interlude.

"All the time," Khynzy admitted. "But once I start playing, it's like the world fades away."

"I get that," Levi nodded. "Music has a way of cutting through the noise."

The atmosphere shifted palpably, the tension in the room pivoting from musical to emotional. Levi gently set down his guitar and met her eyes, an unspoken question lingering in the air.

"You know," he began, his voice wavering slightly, "we make a pretty good team."

"We do," Khynzy agreed, an unfamiliar knot of emotion

tightening in her chest.

"Maybe we should consider making this a regular thing," Levi mused.

With eyes twinkling, yet noticeably softer, Khynzy looked at him. "I'd like that," she whispered. "I'd like that a lot."

Their playing resumed, but both knew they were crafting more than a musical collaboration. They were composing something rare and beautiful, a harmony neither had experienced before.

The rest of the afternoon was a blur of melodies and laughter. When the last echo of the drum and final chord of the guitar hung in the air for the last song, their eyes met, acknowledging a newfound connection neither had anticipated, but both were excited to explore.

Khynzy felt grateful and amazed, not just for the music they'd made but for the unspoken promise of many more harmonies to come—both musical and emotional.

19

The Unspoken Chemistry

Levi walked into the open workspace, immediately noticing that Khynzy's desk was empty. This was unusual for her, especially at this hour. A slight wave of concern washed over him. Approaching Stella, he curbed his curiosity with a casual tone."Hey Stella, do you know where Khynzy is? She's not in her usual spot."

Stella paused her typing and looked up. "She mentioned she'd be at that quiet café down the street. She needed a change of scenery."

"Ah, the calm corner," Levi murmured, aware of the café's reputation as a haven for focused work and thoughtful contemplation.

Pushing open the door of the quiet café, he felt an immediate shift in the air. The aroma of freshly brewed coffee merged harmoniously with the smell of timeworn books, creating an olfactory palette that invoked focus and nostalgia. Soft strains of classical music filled the background, not too loud to distract but just enough to enhance the serene ambience. There were a few patrons scattered around, eyes narrowed over laptops or lost within the pages of a book.

And there she was. Even from a distance, Levi could

identify Khynzy, his eyes instinctively drawn to her medium-brown hair. She sat secluded in a quiet corner, deeply engrossed in her laptop. Next to her laptop sat a ceramic cup, its greenish contents contrasting with the brown and black that dominated the café. It was matcha green tea, her preferred alternative to the ubiquitous coffee.

"Working hard or hardly working?" Levi asked softly, setting his coffee on the table and taking the empty seat opposite her.

Khynzy looked up, her eyes meeting his. "A little bit of both," she replied, her voice tinged with surprise and something warmer. "You stalking me?"

"Just trying to keep my energy up," he chuckled.

"Keeping your energy up? Looks like you're as serious about your drinks as I am," she said, sipping her matcha.

The afternoon light danced through the windows, enveloping them in a soft embrace. They delved into their individual tasks, the silence between them a comfortable companion. Brief exchanges about work and mutual interests punctuated the quietude, their words a subtle dance of shared understandings and unspoken thoughts. The silence of the café wove around them, creating an intimate cocoon, allowing them to exist in their shared silence, a wordless dialogue flowing between them.

Levi, leaning in slightly, couldn't help but suggest, "Is this table open for recurring co-working dates, or is it strictly a solo venture?"

Khynzy met his gaze squarely, a twinkle in her eyes. "I usually value my solitude, but the prospect of a different energy, especially a good one, seems appealing."

"I'll endeavour to be as unobtrusive as a forgotten book on the shelf," he assured her, placing his palm over his heart in a mock pledge.

She laughed, her eyes lingering on his face. "I'll hold you to that, you know."

They returned to their work but under a newly altered dynamic. Each was lost in their tasks, but an acute awareness of the other's presence lingered in the background. It was as though an invisible thread had been tied between them, a silent acknowledgement of the emotional territory they had just ventured into.

As the clock signalled it was time to leave to attend a meeting in the office, Levi reluctantly closed the lid of his laptop. "As much as I'd like to prolong this, duty calls," he announced, somewhat ruefully.

Khynzy looked up, her gaze soft yet piercing. "Leaving me to my solitude and matcha?"

"Wouldn't dream of pulling you away from what you love," he said, zipping his bag. "Same time tomorrow?"

"It's a date," she responded, pausing for dramatic effect. "Well, not a date-date, but you know what I mean."

"Understood perfectly," Levi said, his eyes holding hers for an elongated, tantalising moment.

As Levi stepped out of the café, he felt a subtle but undeniable shift in the air. In a space designed for solitude, he and Khynzy had stumbled upon a different kind of quiet—a quiet teeming with unspoken possibilities.

And it was only a matter of time before they took the plunge.

20

You're Not Alone

Khynzy, engrossed in her computer screen, was immersed in her rigorous software development tasks. The surrounding environment was a muted blur; her focus sharply tuned to her work's intricacies. It was within this cocoon of concentration that a sudden message on her phone broke through.

Her eyes darted between the message and swiftly back to her screen, the words a shadow in her conscious mind, not fully grasped. It wasn't her relentless devotion to her work that made the message hover unacknowledged; it was a protective veil of denial, shielding her from the sadness of those words.

The message was from her aunt, Aunt Mildred. She had been more than just an aunt; she had stepped in as a guardian, a confidante, and a guiding light when Khynzy's parents had been tragically taken from her. The message was simple yet heavy with the weight of emotions that words could barely convey.

Aunt Mildred, who was ten years older than her dad, had taken early retirement in her serene hometown overseas. Khynzy, however, remained tethered to the vibrant city, a place imbued with the precious memories of her parents, an enduring connection to her lost loved ones, compelling her to stay. This emotional anchor heightened the pain of separation, now intensified by the devastating news.

"Zee-zee," it read, "my health is declining rapidly. The doctors have said that my time may be limited. I don't want to be alone in these final moments. Can you come?"

The message struck Khynzy like a thunderbolt on the second read, emotions crashing over her in waves. Her heartache was twofold—Aunt Mildred's illness and the distance that separated them. She had always known that Aunt Mildred was not just a family member but a lifeline, a beacon of unwavering support. The idea of being apart during Aunt Mildred's last moments was unbearable.

With swift determination, Khynzy began the process of filing for emergency leave. Her fingers typed with a sense of urgency, each keystroke fuelled by the deep love and gratitude she held for Aunt Mildred. She crafted an email to her supervisor, her words sincere and filled with the gravity of the situation. She explained that her aunt, her father's sister, Aunt Mildred, was dying overseas, and her presence was desperately needed.

Within minutes, a response arrived—a message of compassion and understanding. Her supervisor expressed sympathy and offered swift approval for the leave request. In a world where work often felt like a relentless treadmill, this empathy reminded Khynzy that she was part of a community that extended beyond the boundaries of her daily tasks.

With a heavy sigh, Khynzy started to gather her belongings. As her colleagues approached, she couldn't help but notice the shifting colours of their auras. Stella's was a soft lavender—gentle and empathetic. The hue seemed to deepen as Stella gently touched Khynzy's shoulder. "Hey, Khynzy, are you alright?"

"I'm doing my best. Just got some difficult news about my aunt..." Khynzy replied, feeling comforted by the stability of Stella's aura.

Tim, who sat a few desks away, chimed in. His aura radiated a sincere blue layered with genuine concern. "I'm really sorry to hear that, Khynzy. Don't hesitate to ask if there's anything we can do for you."

Jennie joined the conversation next. Usually, her aura had green streaks of jealousy and rivalry, but today, it was a surprising blend of yellow and orange—warm and supportive. "Khynzy, we're here for you. If you need to take time off or if there's anything we can help with, just let us know."

Touched by the rare sincerity in Jennie's aura, Khynzy's eyes threatened to spill over with tears. "Thank you, everyone," she said, her voice laden with gratitude. As she looked around, the auras of her colleagues seemed to blend into a temporary tapestry of compassion and friendship. "I'll keep you updated."

❦

Levi's daily stand-up meeting had just finished. He returned to his desk, focused on the tasks before him. His thoughts were suddenly pulled away when he glanced at the screen and saw Khynzy's name in his inbox. Curiosity piqued, he clicked on the message and began to read.

"Emergency leave," he muttered under his breath as he read the contents of the email. Khynzy's words were filled with urgency and love, explaining that her aunt was gravely ill and that she needed to be by her side. Levi's heart clenched as he absorbed the gravity of the situation.

Without hesitation, Levi picked up his phone and dialled Khynzy's number. As the phone rang, his mind raced with thoughts of how he could support her during this challenging time.

"Hello?" Khynzy's voice was a mix of weariness and

determination.

"Khynzy, it's Levi," he said gently. "I just read your email. I'm so sorry to hear about your aunt. How are you holding up?"

There was a brief pause on the other end of the line, and then Khynzy's voice cracked. "It's been tough, Levi. I just want to be there for her."

"I understand," Levi replied. "Listen, I want you to know that I'm here for you. If you need anything—whether it's someone to talk to, someone to drive you somewhere, or anything else—I'm just a call away."

Khynzy's voice was filled with gratitude. "Thank you, Levi. Your offer means a lot to me."

Levi felt a surge of determination. "Khynzy, I will pick you up and take you to the airport. I'll make sure you get there safely."

There was a moment of silence before Khynzy spoke again, her voice soft but filled with emotion. "Levi, you've been so supportive through all of this. I don't know how to thank you."

Levi's heart warmed at her words. "Khynzy, you don't need to thank me. Friends support each other, and I want to be there for you. We'll get through this together."

Tears welled up in Khynzy's eyes, and her voice wavered. "I'm lucky to have a friend like you, Levi."

Levi's voice was steady, filled with reassurance. "And I'm lucky to know someone as strong and caring as you, Khynzy. We'll face whatever comes next, one step at a time."

As they continued to talk, Levi felt a deep connection forming between them—a connection that went beyond their roles as colleagues. At that moment, he realised how much Khynzy meant to him and how important it was to be a source of support during her time of need.

Later that morning, Levi parked his car outside Khynzy's

home. He stepped out of the car and walked up to her front door; his heart filled with concern and determination. When the door opened, Khynzy stood before him, her eyes tired but grateful.

"Thank you for being here, Levi," she said softly.

Levi offered her a warm smile. "Of course, Khynzy. Let's get you to the airport."

As they drove in silence, the weight of the moment hung in the air. Khynzy's aunt's health was delicate, and the journey ahead was uncertain. But amid the uncertainty, there was a sense of solidarity, a shared understanding that they were facing this challenge together.

At the airport, Levi parked the car and turned to Khynzy. "I'll wait here until you're ready to go through security. And when you return, I'll be here to pick you up, no matter the time."

Tears welled up in Khynzy's eyes as she looked at Levi. "I don't know how I would have managed without you."

Levi reached out and gently squeezed her hand. "You're not alone in this, Khynzy. Remember that."

Khynzy nodded, her voice a whisper. "I will."

As Khynzy walked into the airport, Levi watched her until she disappeared from sight. He knew that the journey ahead would be challenging, but he was determined to be a constant source of support for her. In the face of adversity, their bond had deepened, and he was grateful to have Khynzy as a friend—someone who had come to mean so much more to him than he had ever imagined.

❦

As the plane touched down on foreign soil, Khynzy's heart raced with a mixture of emotions. The city's unfamiliarity seemed insignificant compared to the overwhelming need to be by Aunt Mildred's side. She navigated through the airport, her determination unwavering as she made her way to the hospital where her aunt lay, her spirit summoning every ounce of strength to traverse the distance that separated them.

Walking into the hospital room, Khynzy's heart squeezed at the sight before her. Her once robust and lively Aunt Mildred now lay with a fragility that seemed surreal. Her aura, a delicate dance of colours that spoke to the complexities of her life, had shifted into a tapestry of softer shades, as if the energy that had once fuelled her was gently receding.

Khynzy approached the bedside, her voice a soft caress as she greeted Aunt Mildred. Though clouded with illness, her aunt's eyes brightened with recognition and a deep well of love. They held hands, their connection a testament to their bond—a bond that transcended the boundaries of blood and time.

Amid their conversations, as Aunt Mildred's strength wavered but her spirit remained resolute, the topic shifted to matters of the heart. Khynzy's heart ached at the thought that Aunt Mildred's time was limited, yet there was a sense of urgency in their exchange—a desire to share wisdom that transcended the boundaries of life itself.

Aunt Mildred, her voice a gentle whisper, broke the silence. "Zee-zee, my dear, is there someone special in your life?"

Khynzy smiled softly, her heart touched by the tenderness in Aunt Mildred's gaze. "No, Aunt Mildred. I'm not in a relationship right now."

Aunt Mildred's eyes twinkled with a knowing light as if she could read the unspoken thoughts in Khynzy's mind. "You're a beautiful young woman, Zee-zee. Never be afraid to open your heart to love. Life is precious, and it's meant to be shared."

Khynzy's gaze held a mixture of curiosity and vulnerability. "Is that how it was for you and Uncle?"

Aunt Mildred's lips, edged with fine lines, curved into a fond smile. "Yes, dear. Your uncle and I were married late in life. We realised the importance of companionship and building a life together. We didn't have the luxury of time on our side, especially since he passed away early, but we didn't waste a moment."

Khynzy's heart swelled with a mixture of emotions. "Do you think I'll find someone like that?"

Aunt Mildred's hand reached out, clasping Khynzy's with a gentle squeeze. "I believe that love has a way of finding us when we least expect it."

A quiet pause settled between them, the weight of their words mingling with the unspoken truths they both understood. Aunt Mildred's voice, though soft, carried a depth of conviction that resonated within Khynzy's heart.

"Aunt Mildred," Khynzy began, her voice a blend of curiosity and vulnerability, "there is someone I'm both curious and interested in. But I don't know where it might lead."

Aunt Mildred's eyes held a sparkle of encouragement. "That's a beautiful start, my dear. Remember, life is unpredictable, and sometimes the most wonderful journeys begin with a single step."

Khynzy smiled through her tears, the warmth of Aunt Mildred's wisdom washing over her like a soothing embrace. "Thank you, Aunt Mildred."

Aunt Mildred's gaze held Khynzy's, a testament to a love that spanned generations. "And Khynzy, when love finds you, don't hesitate to embrace it fully. Marry early, my dear. Fill your life with the joy of companionship and the laughter of children. Life is a beautiful journey, and love is its most cherished companion."

Aunt Mildred's aura, once a vibrant medley of colours that spoke of joy and vitality, began to shift like a sunset's descent.

It was as if the colours reflected her journey—of the many hues that had painted her life's canvas. Each shade carried whispers of experiences, laughter and sorrow, triumphs and challenges.

One evening, as Khynzy sat by the bed, Aunt Mildred's gaze met hers, an unspoken language that conveyed more than words ever could. It was a gaze that held a lifetime of memories, a testament to the profound love they had shared.

"I'm here, Aunt Mildred," Khynzy whispered, her voice a gentle affirmation. "You're not alone."

Aunt Mildred's eyes, though tired, held a profound sense of gratitude. At that moment, Khynzy realised that her presence was a balm to Aunt Mildred's soul, a presence that chased away the shadows of solitude. Even in the face of mortality, Aunt Mildred's spirit remained resilient, her gaze a reflection of the connection they shared.

As the hours gave way to days, Khynzy held Aunt Mildred's hand as her presence quietly ebbed away. The room was bathed in a stillness that was both heavy and serene. Khynzy's tears fell freely as she held onto Aunt Mildred's hand, feeling the weight of her departure.

Amid the silence, as the world outside continued to spin, Khynzy felt a sense of serenity settle over her. Her aunt's journey had come to an end, but the echoes of their love would forever reverberate in her heart. The room felt like a sacred space, a sanctuary where farewells were whispered and memories were cherished.

In the days that followed Aunt Mildred's passing, Khynzy found solace in the memories they had shared. She realised that her aunt's legacy was not just in the lessons she had taught but in the unwavering love she had given. The colours of Aunt Mildred's aura may have faded, but the imprint of her spirit remained vivid in Khynzy's heart.

21

Echoes of Absence

Levi's gaze was fixed on the computer screen, but the lines of code before him merged into an indistinct cascade of symbols. The rhythmic clacking of keyboards and the occasional bursts of laughter faded into the background. He was adrift in his own world, the usual rhythm of his surroundings falling silent in his ears, his thoughts instead entwined with memories of Khynzy.

Khynzy, who used to be Levi's refuge from others' pessimistic thoughts, had been away for several days, looking after her sick aunt. Her temporary departure cast a hollow emptiness across Levi's once-familiar environment. The usual cacophony of concealed thoughts from those around him diminished into insignificance, drowned out by the resounding echo of her absence. Levi, unmoored without Khynzy's calming presence, found himself navigating through the silent void left in her wake, every moment a stark reminder of the tranquillity and understanding he was missing.

His thoughts drifted back to the times spent with Khynzy, dwelling on the moments he had shared with her—the way her eyes lit up when she spoke about her hobbies, the subtle warmth in her voice when they shared a laugh, her laughter that rippled through the soundproof music room, the glint in her eyes when they exchanged knowing looks at the calm cafe.

He wondered how she was faring, thousands of miles away, in a place he had never been. The constant stream of inner musings that had always surrounded him had turned into an unsettling hush. In its place, the memory of her presence lingered—a blend of curiosity and connection that defied explanation.

Levi leaned back in his chair, the soft sigh that escaped him a testament to his preoccupation. He had always prided himself on his ability to focus, to compartmentalise the symphony of thoughts that cascaded around him. But today, her absence left him strangely untethered, like a conductor in search of a missing note.

A glance at the clock reminded him that the day was drawing to a close. He had accomplished some tasks, but the satisfaction that usually accompanied his achievements felt muted. The enigma of her absence seemed to cast a shadow over even his most mundane accomplishments. He let out another sigh as he packed his things.

❦

The apartment, usually a sanctuary of quiet contemplation, felt strangely empty. Levi glanced at his phone, an involuntary hope igniting within him that he might find a message from her. But the screen remained devoid of any notification. He placed his phone on the coffee table, its screen casting a faint glow.

He settled into the solitude of his living room, his thoughts still adrift in the enigma of Khynzy. He couldn't help but wonder how her days were passing, whether she was finding the strength to support her aunt during her time of need. The unusual restlessness that gripped his mind was a testament to the depth of their connection—stronger than the mere exchange of thoughts.

Levi knew that life, like code, often had moments of ebb and flow. But he sensed that this chapter—marked by Khynzy's absence—was unique. It was a testament to the thread that connected them, the invisible bond that seemed to bridge their individual worlds.

Levi sank into the couch, the soft hum of the living room filling the space around him. A sudden vibration jolted him – a message. His heart raced, hoping for Khynzy's name, but it was Owen: "Hey bro, catching up with the guys. Wanna join?"

He hesitated, the buzz of anticipation fading. Typing a reply, he felt the weight of midweek lethargy. "Sorry, pass. It's midweek, man."

Owen's response came quickly, "OK, but this weekend's a must. No bailing." Levi's fingers danced over the keys, "When have I ever?" A thumbs up and a grin emoji popped up, sealing the conversation. Levi stared at the screen, the light reflecting in his thoughtful eyes.

With a gentle sigh, Levi scrolled through memories trapped behind the glass of his phone, each image a gentle tug on the strings of his lonely heart. He paused at a candid shot from his 23rd birthday, his face alight with genuine joy, his eyes yet to be acquainted with the nuanced pain of missing someone dearly. His fingers lingered on the screen, tracing the outlines of a time before Khynzy, before her absence created a subtle yet pervasive ache within him.

22

You're a Catch

Months ago, when he had turned 23, Levi found himself estranged from an emotion that most in his age group had at least dabbled in: romantic love. His friends navigated relationships, experiencing the highs of new romance and the lows of heartbreak. Meanwhile, Levi felt stuck, imprisoned by his own abilities.

Whenever he felt the initial spark of attraction to someone, his abilities would kick in, often ruining the magic before it even began. With Macy, whom he met at a mutual friend's party, the thought: *I bet I can make him fall for me, then I'll have my pick between him and Phillip. Or I could have both of them*, flashed through her mind. Another woman's thoughts voiced, *He's ruggedly good-looking but not as successful as Marvin*, which halted him in his tracks.

Eunice, warm, generous, and undeniably attractive, had shared what seemed like a genuine connection with Levi. He felt their bond deepening until they walked past a couple on the street. The woman, simple and average in appearance, was beside a notably tall and handsome man. Eunice's gaze subtly flickered, a swift, almost imperceptible shift. Her unspoken thoughts leaked into Levi's consciousness with a bitter sting; *How did she even manage to snag a guy like that? He's clearly out of her league.*

A few steps further, they passed a shorter and heavier man engrossed in a book at a nearby café. Eunice caught his brief, distracted glance in her direction. Her internal voice was immediately dismissive. *Does he think he stands a chance? Not in this lifetime.*

Levi felt a pang of disappointment. The stark contrast between Eunice's outward warmth and the judgmental nature of her inner thoughts deeply troubled him. The allure he once felt for her began to wane rapidly.

Such experiences accumulated, each serving as a poignant reminder of the double-edged sword his abilities represented. With every disillusionment, his emotional barriers fortified, and his doubts deepened. Could genuine love ever intertwine with his capabilities? Indeed, many women harboured thoughts that are less negative compared to others, thoughts he could potentially overlook. Yet, their lack of depth or dissimilarity with him failed to ignite the spark of interest within him, leaving him wandering in the labyrinth of his solitude, questioning the possibility of a shared journey.

His friend Marco once commented, "Levi, you're such a catch. I don't get why you're still single." If only he knew that Levi's gifts made romantic engagements a field of emotional landmines.

Levi couldn't switch off his abilities, even if he wanted to. He was always aware, always tuned into the undercurrent of negative thoughts around him. This 'gift' felt more like a curse when it came to intimacy; he was forever bound to know the doubts and reservations others had about him, no matter how minor they might be.

During a casual evening with friends, his buddy Owen asked, "Man, what's the holdup? You've got so much going for you."

Levi forced a smile, "I haven't found the right one, I guess."

Steve chuckled, "Man, with your charm, you could have anyone you wanted!"

Levi took a sip of his drink, contemplating his response. "It's not as simple as that," he finally said, leaving his friends puzzled but deciding not to elaborate.

In his quieter moments, Levi fantasised about his ideal type—a woman who was genuinely good at her core, intellectually stimulating, and passionate about her own interests. She would be someone who took care of herself, not just in appearance but in mind and spirit, someone who had interests beyond the superficial—maybe she loved to paint, was an avid reader, or volunteered at an animal shelter. He was looking for someone whose thoughts and actions were congruent, a person who could offer him peace and quiet in his mind but also stimulate him in ways that made him long for her presence.

As time went by, Levi's sense of isolation expanded. Would he ever experience love without the backdrop of subconscious reservations or flaws? Could he ever find someone whose thoughts—no matter how fleeting or insignificant—wouldn't deter him from taking the leap?

For Levi, the question wasn't whether a suitable partner existed but whether his abilities would forever isolate him from a genuine romantic connection. Until he found a way to reconcile with this aspect of himself, love remained a picture he could look at but never touch.

23

Unspoken Echoes

Levi reclined on his couch, lost in thought. The events of the past few days had woven a tapestry of absence and yearning within him, leaving an indelible mark on his usually composed demeanour. The subtle hum of his phone disrupted the silence, jolting him from his reverie.

His heart skipped a beat as he reached for his phone, fingers trembling with anticipation. A text message illuminated the screen, and his eyes quickly scanned the words, relief flooding his being. It was from Khynzy. She had reached out—a bridge across the chasm of her absence.

"Hey Levi," the message read. "Just wanted to let you know that I'll be flying back tomorrow. Can't wait to be back at the office. See you soon!"

A warmth spread through Levi's chest, a mix of happiness and reassurance that Khynzy was safe and on her way back. The thread that connected them, the undercurrent of understanding he had grown accustomed to, felt renewed in that moment. He typed a quick response, fingers flying across the keyboard.

"Hey Khynzy! That's great news. What time is your flight arriving?" he sent back.

Her reply came swiftly: "Landing at 5 PM."

"Perfect, I'll be there to pick you up from the airport. Safe travels!" Levi typed, his heart light with anticipation.

The words were sent into the digital realm, a simple exchange that carried a depth of emotions he couldn't articulate. As the night deepened, Levi's mind was consumed with thoughts of their impending reunion. He imagined the relief that would wash over him when he saw her, a living testament to her safe return.

However, a promise lingered in the back of Levi's mind. He had agreed to help his friend Owen scout potential properties for his expanding rental business the next day. A commitment he never thought he'd need to break until now.

Picking up his phone again, Levi hesitated momentarily before dialling Owen's number.

"Hey, Owen... Look, I need to cancel our plans tomorrow. Something came up," Levi's voice quivered slightly, betraying the calm he was trying to portray.

Owen's laugh resonated from the phone, casual and teasing, "Levi, cancelling? Did hell freeze over and nobody told me?"

Levi's slight chuckle was empty. "No, I just... I need to pick up a friend from the airport."

Suspicion coloured Owen's tone, "A friend or a 'friend'? Have I met them before?"

"You've seen her at the casino. The one with the ridiculous winning streak that night," Levi offered, trying to remain nonchalant.

Recognition flashed in Owen's voice, "Ah, so it's her. The one you couldn't take your eyes off? I knew it! She's your type, isn't she?"

Levi sighed, a mixture of frustration and vulnerability in his voice. "Look, it's not like that. We're friends. But she's going through a hard time. Her aunt had just died. I want to be there for her."

Owen's demeanour softened, sensing the sincerity in Levi's voice. "I'm sorry to hear that. So, what time is her flight arriving?"

"5 PM," Levi responded quietly.

Owen was momentarily silent, then blurted, "5 PM? Levi, we'd finish property scouting by 3 PM at the latest! You could still make it."

Levi's thoughts vacillated between his friend and the woman who unwittingly occupied a special place in his life. "It's not just about being at the airport, Owen. I want to do something meaningful for her. She's had it really rough, and she's… well, she's become really important to me."

The playful tease was evident even through the phone. "Sounds like she's more than just a friend, huh?"

Levi dodged the insinuation. "That's beside the point, Owen. She needs a friend right now, and I want to be that for her."

A hint of seriousness lined Owen's voice. "Alright, I get it. But how about you give me until 2 PM? We power through the properties, and you're free to support her however you need, yeah?"

After a moment's contemplation, Levi agreed, "Fine, but I'm leaving at exactly 2 PM, Owen. Not a minute later."

Owen attempted one last inquiry. "Hey, do you mind if I come with you to the airport afterwards? Maybe grab a coffee while we wait?"

Levi, firm but gentle, declined, "I appreciate it, but I think she'll need something familiar. This has to be just me, Owen."

Accepting the boundary, Owen concluded, "Understood, man. Just trying to offer some support. Let's knock out those properties, and then you go do what you need to do."

Levi's mind wandered as he hung up the call, imagining Khynzy's face when she sees him waiting at the arrivals hall.

His thoughts also ventured towards Stella, Khynzy's effervescent best friend at work.

Taking out his phone again, he texted Stella, "You probably already know Khynzy is coming back tomorrow evening. I'm picking her up. Could we possibly bring her to your place? I thought being with you might bring her some comfort and normalcy after everything that's happened."

Moments later, Stella's reply popped up. "Absolutely, Levi. You're so thoughtful. She'll need her friends now more than ever. Let's make it a quiet, comforting evening for her. Any favourite dish of hers I should cook?"

Levi pondered briefly before responding, "She's always raved about your spinach and ricotta lasagna. Let's keep it simple, though. I'll bring some wine."

With plans taking shape, Levi found himself amidst a flurry of emotions, carefully balancing the sadness he felt for Khynzy's loss and the gentle spark that flickered whenever he thought of her.

24

Whispers and Wanderings

Owen, ever the enthusiast with a nose for opportunity, firmly believed in expanding his burgeoning rental empire. His trust in Levi, though rooted in tangible success, was blissfully unaware of the silent symphony of thoughts that swirled around his friend.

Levi walked alongside Owen, his face betraying no emotion as they approached the ageing apartment complex, its faded brick walls whispering stories of decades gone by. Owen's eyes sparkled with excitement and potential profit, completely oblivious to the cacophony of unseen doubts swarming around Levi's senses.

Levi's gift - or curse, depending on perspective - was a secret well-guarded. He could hear the dark, insecure thoughts that people hid behind polite smiles and firm handshakes. As he listened to Owen's enthusiastic plans for the ageing building, he focused on the real estate agent beside them, silently anticipating the internal murmurs of dissent that he'd inevitably pick up.

There's likely mould in the walls, an anxious thought from the agent filtered through, clear and distinct amidst the din of concealed concerns. Levi's eyes subtly shifted towards the damp, shadowy corners of the brickwork, never letting on.

"You know," Levi began, interrupting Owen's animated interior planning, "it might be a good idea to get a mould inspection done before making any decisions. This place is pretty old, and we might face issues during renovation if there's mould."

Owen paused, evaluating Levi's words, before finally nodding. His trust in Levi, blind yet unyielding, had always been a warm yet painful reminder of the thick veil of secrecy between them.

As they continued their tour, Levi intercepted more hidden reservations from the agent, guiding Owen away from potential pitfalls with gentle suggestions and cautious insights. Each word was a calculated move to protect his friend without revealing the unseen world that screamed into Levi's ears with every step.

In a moment of solitude, as Owen wandered into one of the potential apartments, entranced by the view of the bustling city below, Levi took a quiet second for himself. He wondered, as he often did, whether the truth would fortify their friendship or shatter the trust that had been so carefully constructed over the years.

Owen, oblivious to the emotional storm brewing inside his friend, threw an arm around Levi in a brotherly embrace. "Man, I don't know how you do it, but you always seem to catch things no one else does. I'm lucky to have you, bro."

Levi mustered a smile, clapping his hand on Owen's back, while the concealed thoughts of doubt and deceit echoed around him. His secret remained safe, barricaded behind a fortress of loving deception.

The next property was awash with sunlight, with vast, open windows showcasing a breathtaking panoramic view of the city skyline. While outwardly praising the spectacular view, the agent silently thought, *I hope they don't notice the *structural problem with these windows.**

Levi, peering critically at the large panes, interjected cautiously, "Owen, perhaps we should consider the potential maintenance costs of these windows, especially given the building's age. They provide a stunning view but might become a liability in the future."

Owen paused, his gaze torn between the enchanting cityscape and the potentially problematic windows, then nodded appreciatively at Levi's insight, and they proceeded to the next viewing.

The third property was an outdated yet quaint unit nestled on the outskirts of the downtown area. It lacked the modern charm of the previous properties but held a certain warm ambience that was undeniably appealing. This time, Levi picked up desperation from the agent's thoughts.

I must sell this as quickly as possible, but if they detect my urgency, my commission will dwindle, the agent worried internally, eyes darting nervously towards the semi-packed boxes.

Smiling lightly, he nudged Owen. "This place has a lot of potential, don't you think? Plus, I sense that we might be able to negotiate a very favourable deal here. There's a chance the owner might be in a hurry to close."

Owen's eyebrows lifted, his interest piqued by the potential bargain. After a healthy back-and-forth, they managed to secure the unit for a price significantly below market value, all thanks to Levi's hidden insights.

He looked at Levi, a sincere warmth in his eyes. "You know, I'd be lost in this without you, Levi. Your instincts... they're something else."

Levi's smile was genuine, but hidden behind it was a delicate cradle of secrets, rocking gently between the bonds of friendship and the silent screams of hidden truths. Casting a covert glance at his wristwatch, he noted the time: 1:55 p.m. A mental note tugged at him—he had only five minutes left before he had promised to excuse himself. Khynzy's flight wouldn't touch down until 5:00 p.m., yet his heart thrummed in his chest with an eagerness to simply be present when she arrived.

Lightly injecting into the amiable conversation, he offered, "Owen, I'm afraid I have to get going. I need to be at the airport soon."

Owen chuckled warmly, a knowing smile dancing in his eyes. "Ah, the unspoken romance of the airport pickup. Khynzy will surely appreciate it, especially after such a trying time abroad," he replied teasingly but with a gentle understanding.

Levi could only manage a soft, somewhat shy smile in response, acknowledging the unspoken feelings he harboured for his colleague. Under the playful jest, Owen acknowledged the depth of the situation, respecting Levi's unvoiced emotions and Khynzy's recent loss.

As Levi navigated the route to the airport, his mind was a torrent of juxtaposed thoughts, torn between the soothing comfort he wished to provide Khynzy and the moral dilemma he'd entwined himself with regarding Owen.

25

You've Been Missed

The drive to the airport was a mixture of excitement and impatience, the cityscape whizzing by in a blur. The airport terminal came into view, a bustling hub of arrivals and departures.

Levi arrived at the airport earlier than necessary, a blend of excitement and anxiety emanating from him. His eyes remained glued to his phone app, repeatedly refreshing to check the status of Khynzy's flight. When it finally switched to 'Landed', his heart leapt, propelling him out of his car.

Making his way to the arrival area, the rhythmic tapping of his fingers against his thigh mirrored the anxious beat of his heart, all while the chaotic symphony of the airport unfolded around him. He waited, eyes darting through the emerging sea of faces until they settled on her. Khynzy, still immensely captivating, emerged amidst the travellers. Her smile, genuine yet shadowed with a subtle sorrow, locked onto his, momentarily dispersing the shadows clouding his thoughts. As he stepped forward, a cascade of emotions tumbled within him.

"Hey Levi," she whispered, her voice a sad melody.

He wrapped her in a warm, comforting hug. Khynzy sank

into the embrace, the kindness in the gesture providing a fragile warmth amid her grief. A soft sigh whispered her unspoken thanks as she leaned into him, finding a momentary haven from her pain. As they parted slightly, Levi looked into her eyes, his own reflecting a gentle sorrow. "I'm so sorry for your loss, Khynzy," he whispered.

A glimmer of appreciation flickered through her tear-brimmed eyes. "Thank you, Levi," she replied, her voice catching slightly in her throat. "It's really good to see you."

Eventually, they found themselves within the comforting walls of Stella's apartment. Stella, ever considerate, had prepared a welcome-back dinner, a thoughtful gesture Levi hoped would offer Khynzy an additional layer of solace and familiar comfort in these trying times.

Stella's infectious laughter filled the air as she embraced Khynzy tightly. "Welcome back, you wanderer! We missed you around here."

Khynzy's smile was genuine, a reflection of the gratitude she felt for the friends who had been a pillar of support during her absence. "Thank you, Stella. It's good to be back."

As they settled around the dining table, their conversations flowed seamlessly, a mixture of catching up and sharing stories from their time apart. Khynzy recounted her journey, the bittersweet moments she had shared with her aunt, and the support she had been able to provide. Stella's presence provided a sense of normalcy that Khynzy welcomed, and Levi found himself drawn into the easy camaraderie that defined their interactions.

As dinner came to an end, Levi offered to drive Khynzy home. They said their goodbyes to Stella and headed out to the car. Once inside, Khynzy turned to Levi, her eyes filled with warmth and gratitude.

"I really appreciate you picking me up from the airport and giving me a ride home, Levi. It means a lot to me."

Levi smiled, locking eyes with her. "Of course, Khynzy. I'm glad you're back."

"You've been missed," he said sincerely, capturing the essence of what they were both feeling.

In that confined space, the unspoken connection between them seemed to crystallise. As they drove, the atmosphere was charged with a silent understanding that transcended the need for words.

26

Until the Spring, Let's Pretend

The ride back from Stella's place was quiet, filled with a reflective silence. Khynzy stared out of the car window; her gaze focused on the passing scenery, lost in thought. Levi parked his car outside Khynzy's house. The weight of the silence was palpable, echoing the turmoil of recent events. As they stepped out into the cool evening air, Levi broke the silence with a gentle suggestion, "How about playing a song? It might help." His voice carried a warmth, an unspoken understanding of the solace they found in music.

Khynzy gave a slight nod, her eyes mirroring a mix of gratitude and deep sorrow. Together, they walked to her music room, a space that had started to capture the essence of their musical hobby. Levi's guitar, left there since their first jam session, stood in the corner, symbolising the newfound aspect of their friendship where music had become a comforting and shared interest.

Despite not planning to stream, Khynzy instinctively reached for her brown bag mask adorned with whimsical panda eyes. It had transformed from a mere streaming accessory into a symbol of her emotional armour, a shield that allowed her to confront her inner turmoil while shielding her vulnerability from the world.

Once settled in the music room, Levi gently picked up his guitar. "Let's play 'Until the Spring, Let's Pretend'," he suggested, his fingers lightly caressing the guitar strings. It's a song from Lynn's Rebellion, a band known for their rich alternative rock melodies, weaving introspective lyrics with dynamic compositions. Their music often delves into themes of loss, hope, and resilience, with each song portraying a journey through the complexities of human emotion.

As Levi began to strum the guitar, a gentle yet meaningful melody filled the room, crafting a soundscape that was both soothing and contemplative. His voice, raw and sincere, rose and fell with the chords, imbuing the lyrics with an emotional depth that resonated within the walls of the music room:

♪ *Grey skies cover me, I feel alone,*
Without you, both winter days and nights feel long,
Though in my heart, a flicker of light has shown,
A brighter day is yet to dawn. ♪

Khynzy, sitting behind her drums, felt a connection to each word. As the chorus neared, she raised her drumsticks, her movements deliberate yet filled with a quiet intensity. Her drums joined the guitar, the beats powerful yet controlled, adding a layer of depth and emotion to the song. Together, they created an atmosphere imbued with the energy and spirit of alternative rock, deeply personal and evocative:

♪ *When the hard times come to an end,*
When the sun's warmth is around the bend,
Hold me close, help me mend,
Until the spring, let's pretend,
Until the spring, let's pretend. ♪

Behind her mask, tears began to well up in Khynzy's eyes, hidden from view yet profoundly felt. The music, a perfect blend of guitar riffs and rhythmic drumming, was a testament to their shared journey—a journey through the shifting tides of sorrow and the emerging glimmers of hope.

As they neared the song's conclusion, Khynzy's drumming gently faded into silence, her sticks coming to a rest. Levi's voice softened, carrying the final words with a tenderness that echoed in the now-still room:

♪ *To the stars, I softly speak,*
For the strength, for the peace I seek,
In the spring, no more despair,
In its light, pretence dissolves in the air. ♪

In the profound silence that followed, Levi set his guitar aside and approached Khynzy, who remained seated on her drum throne. He gently pulled her into an embrace, her head resting against his chest. Hidden behind her panda-eyed mask, Khynzy allowed herself to sob quietly, her tears a release of the emotions she had held back for so long. Levi held her, offering silent comfort and understanding. In his arms, she found not just a friend but a companion who shared her love for music and understood the depth of her pain. They shared a moment in the dimly lit room, united in their silent strength, bonded by the rhythm and melodies of their friendship and the healing power of music.

27

It's Called Jealousy

The office hummed with the familiar rhythm of keyboards clicking and muted conversations as Khynzy stepped through the doorway. After the emotional journey she had undertaken, returning to her work routine felt both grounding and comforting. She exchanged smiles and greetings with her colleagues, each interaction a reminder of the friendships she cherished.

However, amidst the familiar faces, a new presence caught her attention. A young man with tousled golden brown hair and an eager smile was engrossed in a conversation with one of the team leads. His enthusiasm was evident, and Khynzy's curiosity was piqued as she caught snippets of their conversation.

"...new developer, Doug," the team lead explained, nodding toward the newcomer. "Just joined us, fresh from his previous project."

Khynzy's eyes met Doug's as he turned in her direction, a genuine smile lighting up his face. Her warm smile in return was polite, her curiosity about the new colleague growing. As the day progressed, she found herself drawn into conversations with him and the rest of the team. His excitement was infectious, and Khynzy appreciated the fresh perspective he brought.

However, as the days passed, it became evident that Doug's interest in her extended beyond professional camaraderie. He was attentive and openly admiring, showering her with compliments and often lingering in her vicinity. His intentions were unmistakable, and while Khynzy was flattered by his attention, she found herself navigating unfamiliar territory.

Levi, who often comes out of the meeting room close to the Code squad's area, noticed the change in dynamics. Doug's interactions with Khynzy were marked by an overt affection that couldn't be ignored. Levi's own emotions, usually kept under a veil of stoicism, began to stir. He found himself scrutinising their exchanges, an unexplainable tension coiling within him.

One afternoon, as Khynzy was engrossed in a discussion with Doug about a new project, Levi's curiosity got the best of him. He found himself eavesdropping on their conversation, his heightened senses picking up on the nuances of their exchange. Doug's infatuation was palpable, and it didn't escape Levi's notice that Khynzy was handling the situation with her usual grace and poise.

As Khynzy excused herself to continue her work, Levi approached her desk, a casual smile masking his internal turmoil. "Seems like you've made quite an impression on Doug."

Khynzy chuckled softly, her gaze meeting Levi's. "He's friendly, that's for sure."

Levi's eyes held a mixture of amusement and something he couldn't quite pinpoint. "More than friendly, I'd say."

Khynzy arched an eyebrow, her curiosity piqued. "You're being cryptic, Levi."

Levi's smile was wry, his fingers tapping a rhythm on the

edge of her desk. "Just an observation. It's hard to miss."

Khynzy's lips twitched into a knowing smile, her gaze briefly turning toward Doug before returning to Levi. "Well, you know how these things go. Sometimes, some people are just more expressive."

Levi's expression remained unreadable, but a hint of something resembling unease flickered in his eyes. "Expressive, huh?"

Khynzy chuckled softly, her voice gentle. "Don't worry, Levi. It's harmless."

Levi nodded, the tension within him not entirely abating. "If you say so."

As the days continued, Doug's unabashed pursuit of Khynzy remained a constant presence. Despite her reassurances, Levi found himself grappling with a surge of emotions he couldn't entirely suppress. He watched as Doug's attentions continued, their interactions bordering on overt flirtation.

One evening, as the office began to empty, Khynzy settled at her desk, absorbed in finalising her tasks. Levi, exiting a just-concluded meeting, felt his attention drift towards her direction, almost magnetically. At that moment, Doug made his way to Khynzy's desk, clutching a vivid bouquet of flowers—a delicate array of roses and lilies, their fragrance filling the air.

"Hey, Khynzy," Doug began, trying to sound nonchalant, but the tremor in his voice betrayed him. "A friend of mine, a florist, has been going through a tough time financially. I thought of buying these to help out, and well, I reckoned you might like them." His eyes met hers, holding a hint of deeper feelings he wasn't ready to voice yet.

Khynzy's face lit up, her appreciation evident. "They're beautiful, Doug. Thank you." The flowers added a soft glow to her workspace, reflecting the colours dancing around

Doug. The vibrant hues of the flowers seemed to echo Doug's emotions as his aura shimmered in radiant pinks, passionate reds, and touches of gleaming gold.

Levi, a silent observer, clenched his jaw. His ability allowed him to hear the unsaid, the concealed thoughts of others. Yet, from Doug, he sensed no deceit or ulterior motives, only pure adoration for Khynzy. This unblemished sincerity was alien to Levi and deeply troubling in its own right.

As Doug retreated, a parting glance shared with Khynzy, Levi felt a sinking sensation in his gut. In a world saturated with hidden agendas and masked intentions, Doug's genuine gesture was an enigma that left him profoundly unsettled.

Levi couldn't shake the unease that had settled within him. His interactions with Khynzy had always been marked by an unspoken understanding, a connection that transcended words. And now, a new element had entered the equation, stirring emotions he had never quite explored.

Later, as Khynzy was about to leave the office, she found Doug waiting for her by the lift. Levi was also there, seemingly engrossed in his phone.

"Doug, you're still here?" she asked, her eyes catching the shades of anticipation in his aura.

"I heard about this amazing concert happening this weekend," Doug said, his aura shimmering with a mix of excitement and hope. "Would you like to go watch it with me?"

Before Khynzy could respond, her phone buzzed. A text message from Levi appeared on her screen: "Don't go."

Startled, Khynzy spun her head towards Levi. He looked up from his phone at the exact moment, and their eyes met in a swift, intense exchange. Her heart raced as she held his gaze briefly, a question forming in her mind. *Could he be jealous?*

Taking a deep breath, Khynzy turned back to Doug, feeling the need to respond. Doug's aura, still hopeful, seemed to waver, picking up on the sudden shift in atmosphere. "Sorry, Doug, I appreciate the invitation, " she said with a regretful smile, "but I'm going to have to pass this time."

Doug's aura dulled for a moment, but he recovered quickly, managing a smile. "No worries, maybe some other time."

As Doug walked away, Khynzy turned to Levi. "I do like that band, you know."

Levi met her gaze, his eyes softening. "Then I'll take you to the concert."

Khynzy's eyes widened in surprise. "But how? The tickets are probably sold out by now."

Levi grinned, the tension from earlier dissipating. "For you, I'll find a way. Consider it a surprise. I'll pick you up for dinner at six tomorrow, and then we can head to the concert together."

28

Night of Anticipation

The next day, Khynzy's anticipation for the evening ahead was undeniable. She couldn't help but feel a mixture of excitement and nervousness as she prepared for her night out with Levi. Their relationship had always been complex, and she didn't want to assume anything, afraid of the possibility of disappointment or rejection.

Levi arrived to pick her up precisely at six, dressed smartly and wearing a confident smile. Khynzy greeted him with a warm smile, a sense of ease settling over her as they exchanged greetings.

"Ready for a great night?" Levi asked as he opened the car door for her.

Khynzy nodded, her excitement bubbling up. "Absolutely. I've been looking forward to this."

Seated at a sophisticated restaurant, the atmosphere buzzed with the clinking of glassware and murmurings of conversations. As they enjoyed their dinner, Khynzy couldn't help but scan the crowd. Her eyes decoded the spectrum of auras, absorbing the myriad of emotions that filled the room —enthusiastic fans, cheerful friends, and loving couples.

Meanwhile, Levi had a different layer of perception. He

picked up on the negative thoughts that crossed people's minds, an unintentional eavesdropping that came with his unique ability. It was like an undercurrent of whispers running beneath the visible world, each thought was another drop in an ocean of secrets.

Eventually, the pair found themselves amidst the energetic crowd at the concert venue. The atmosphere was charged with excitement, every face in the crowd a portrait of anticipation.

As they navigated through the crowd, the space became increasingly crowded. Levi couldn't shake the fear of being separated from Khynzy in the throng of people. Without consciously thinking, he reached out and casually took her hand in his.

The moment their fingers intertwined, a rush of warmth washed over Levi. It was a simple gesture, one that friends might make to stay connected in a crowd, but it held a deeper significance for him. He realised that he didn't want to let go.

As they continued moving toward a spot with a decent view of the stage, Levi couldn't help but glance at Khynzy. Her face was lit up with excitement, her eyes twinkling in the colourful glow from the stage as she moved subtly to the beat of the lively music. It was at this moment that he fully recognised the depth of his feelings for her.

But a soft worry began to knit his brow. His unique ability to hear negative thoughts had always built a wall between him and others. Yet, with Khynzy, it was different; her presence was like a quiet harbour in the storm of other people's negativity. He found something special in her, something he feared he might never find again.

Levi felt a dilemma bubble up inside him as they held hands. Should he let go of her hand? Was holding hands blurring the lines of their friendship? He grappled with these questions internally but decided to keep their hands intertwined.

He opted to navigate this delicate situation cautiously, not wanting to rush and potentially ruin their rare connection. Levi chose to tread lightly, savouring the sweetness of their growing bond and hoping it would blossom into something more in its own time.

Their hands, gently interlocked, became a steady constant amidst the rocking pulse of the concert. Khynzy, her fingers faintly tapping against Levi's in tune with the drummer's potent beats, lost herself in the percussive artistry displayed on stage. Her eyes, alight with both appreciation for the skill before her and the newfound warmth by her side, occasionally darted towards Levi, ensuring the silent, tender thread between them remained unbroken. On the other hand, Levi found his attention split between the expressive dance of the lead guitarist's fingers on the strings and the soft, rhythmic squeezes from Khynzy's hand that whispered quietly of the connection taking root in the charged concert atmosphere.

Amidst a soulful ballad, their eyes met, holding a conversation deeper and more intricate than words could convey. Around them, the crowd swayed, their mobile lights creating a shimmering ocean of stars that cradled their unspoken words and the gentle promise lingering in their connected fingers. Even as the concert's energy peaked again with a lively, electric number, their hands remained steadfastly intertwined, a silent anchor in the sea of sonic waves washing over them.

Driving Khynzy home after the concert, Levi's car hummed softly as it pulled up in front of her apartment. The atmosphere within the vehicle was palpable. The night's excitement still flushed her cheeks as she turned to Levi, her eyes glistening with gratitude.

"Thank you so much, Levi," she said, her voice soft and

sincere. "Tonight was incredible. Dinner, the concert—I can't believe you managed to get those tickets. You've made this night truly special."

Levi's eyes, warm and filled with affection, locked onto hers. He could feel his heart pounding in his chest as he looked at her, her lips invitingly close. His desire to kiss her was nearly overpowering, but he fought to maintain his composure. He didn't want to rush things; he wanted this connection to grow naturally.

"You're more than welcome, Khynzy," Levi replied, his voice tinged with a hint of longing. "I'm just glad you enjoyed it. You deserve all the happiness in the world."

Their eyes remained locked for a moment, a magnetic pull drawing them closer. But then, with great effort, Levi leaned back slightly in his seat, breaking the intense connection.

"It's getting late," he said, his voice husky. "You should head inside. I don't want you to be tired tomorrow."

Khynzy nodded, a mixture of disappointment and anticipation in her eyes. "You're right. I should get some rest."

She opened the car door but hesitated for a moment, looking back at Levi. "Levi, thank you again. This was one of the best nights of my life."

Levi smiled his feelings for her growing stronger by the second. "I'm glad to hear that, Khynzy. Goodnight."

With a final, lingering gaze, Khynzy stepped out of the car and closed the door behind her. Levi watched as she walked towards her apartment building, his heart still pounding. He knew he had made the right decision to take things slowly, to savour the moments they shared. And as he drove away, he couldn't help but feel that this was just the beginning of something beautiful.

❦

Lying in bed, Khynzy replayed the evening's events. The night with Levi had been nothing short of magical, adorned with laughter and a connection that seemed to traverse beyond the mundane. Yet, her mind lingered on the unresolved tension from their almost-kiss in the car, leaving her heart in confusion.

"What are we, exactly?" Khynzy murmured into the stillness of her dark room. At the concert, their fingers had danced into an entwined embrace, souls intertwining as the music cascaded around them. A magnetic pull tethered her to him. Yet, when the universe gifted them the perfect moment to kiss, he hesitated, as though restrained by an unseen force.

She couldn't decipher him. Khynzy, who could usually perceive the colours of emotion swirling around individuals, found Levi to be an exception, his aura invisible to her discerning eyes. This peculiar inability nagged at her, particularly now when understanding his emotions could untangle the web of uncertainty that she found herself caught in.

Was his hesitation a reflection of uncertainty or a deliberate pause to allow their connection to simmer slowly? In a world where she could usually find answers in the vibrant hues of people's auras, Levi's invisible emotional spectrum left her grappling with the intangible. If only she could peer into his aura, perhaps the colours swirling therein would give her clarity about his feelings that now eluded her.

As her thoughts spun ceaselessly, she conceded that sleep would remain elusive. A sigh escaped Khynzy's lips, recognising that the answers to the questions dancing in her mind would not present themselves that night. She softly chuckled, foreseeing the panda eyes that would undoubtedly greet her in the morning mirror. It was her whimsical term for the dark circles that appeared beneath her eyes after nights like this one, where sleep was traded for a cascade of ponderings.

29

The Interloper

Khynzy stepped into the office cafeteria, a plate of salad and a cup of matcha green tea in hand. She spotted Doug waving at her from a table near the windows.

"Hey, Khynzy, over here!" Doug called out.

His aura differed from those she was used to — bright, almost radiant, with passionate red and ambitious orange hues that seemed to scream, "Look at me!" He was undeniably attractive and carried himself with a confident ease that was hard to ignore, but a bit too bulky for Khynzy's taste.

As they chatted over lunch, Khynzy learned more about Doug. He enjoys working out, is an avid rock climber, and has a soft spot for rescue dogs. He spoke openly about his life, sprinkling in just the right amount of charm and humour. It was hard not to be taken by his charismatic energy.

Levi entered the cafeteria, his eyes scanning the room for Khynzy. Stella, who was looking for a seat, spotted him.

"Looking for someone?" Stella quipped as she approached him.

Levi sighed, "Am I that transparent?"

"As a freshly cleaned window," Stella retorted.

Just then, Levi's gaze settled on Khynzy and Doug, laughing about something. Under his breath, he muttered, "Bad Doug," and turned to leave the cafeteria. "Actually, I've lost my appetite," he told Stella.

❦

Later that day, Levi attended a meeting with various department heads to discuss staffing needs. A squad from another office was urgently in need of a developer.

"If anyone has suggestions, feel free to speak up," the project manager encouraged.

Usually, Levi could hear people's negative thoughts and subtly inject his own ideas in response. But at that moment, silence filled his mind; no negative thoughts emerged from the attendees.

Where are those damn negative thoughts when you need them?! He muttered to himself. Left with no other option, he voiced his recommendation aloud.

"How about Doug from the Code squad? He's got a strong background, and I think he'd be a great fit. Plus, since he is outgoing and he just recently transferred to the Code squad, he'll be able to adjust to another new team easily." Levi suggested.

The project manager jotted down the suggestion. "Excellent idea. I'll take it up with HR."

Exiting the meeting, Levi wrestled with his conscience. Although he told himself he had made a professional recommendation—Doug was unquestionably qualified—he couldn't shake the feeling that his emotions had influenced his decision.

❦

Khynzy sensed a shift in the atmosphere when she returned to her desk. Doug walked over, visibly disappointed, his usually vibrant aura unexpectedly tinged with murky grey. "Looks like I will be re-assigned to another squad. In another office building, no less."

"Really?" she asked, a mixture of emotions flooding her.

"Yeah, it came out of nowhere," Doug sighed. "But hey, we can still catch up. It's not like I'm leaving the city."

"Of course," Khynzy replied as Doug walked away.

❦

That evening, Khynzy approached Levi. "I heard they might transfer Doug. Did you suggest it?"

"Yes," Levi admitted, meeting her gaze.

For a moment, silence hung in the air, heavy with unspoken feelings and questions.

"Well, let's hope it's for the best," Khynzy finally said, walking away.

As she left, Levi felt like he had crossed an unspoken boundary, leaving him tangled in a complicated web of professional and personal desires.

30

New Routines

Ever since Doug's transfer, Levi felt unburdened. It was as if a lingering fog had lifted, revealing a sunnier disposition within himself. He attributed this newfound sense of ease to his increased closeness to Khynzy. And close they had grown indeed.

Their casual interactions at the office escalated into more significant, frequent exchanges, making lunchtime an essential part of their days. Sometimes, they would find themselves in the office cafeteria, discussing music or art and contemplating songs for their next jam session. Levi would share his love for vintage cameras, while Khynzy would passionately describe her fascination with abstract art. Their conversations would seamlessly float between office gossip, the latest in music, and the underrated beauty of mundane things. On more adventurous days, they'd escape to a local restaurant, moments that Levi particularly relished. Whether Khynzy was laughing at his jokes or he was captivated by her insights, he treasured these windows into her world.

But the lunches weren't the only moments Levi cherished. On Tuesdays and Thursdays, he'd make it a point to surprise Khynzy with a matcha frappe infused with hazelnut syrup—

her guilty pleasure. He'd arrive at her desk, drink in hand, catching her in the middle of a project or during a conference call.

"I'm trying to limit my sugar intake, you know," Khynzy would declare, an amused smile stretching across her face as she accepted the drink.

"A little indulgence is the spice of life," he'd retort, a familiar twinkle lighting up his eyes.

Khynzy had always valued her privacy and solitude. Before she met Levi, it was mainly Stella who would coax her into embracing the outside world more frequently. Identifying as an ambivert, Khynzy would often need to recharge after periods of social interaction. However, Levi seemed to be an exception. With him, she experienced a unique sense of comfort; his presence didn't seem to sap her social energy.

She shared parts of her life she seldom spoke of, divulging her childhood dreams and hopes for the future. She also became an avid listener, absorbing Levi's musings about his aspirations and his narratives from days gone by. She learned about the resilience of his parents, who maintained their unity despite grappling with financial adversities during his youth.

A day hadn't passed without a conversation between them. These dialogues were often the highlight of their workdays, serving as miniature oases of connection in a sea of corporate monotony. What neither of them could articulate, but both deeply felt, was the magnetic pull that drew them toward each other, filling spaces within them they hadn't known were empty.

On one memorable Thursday, Levi hesitated longer than usual after delivering her favourite frappe. "There's a new movie out this weekend. Would you be interested in going?" he asked, cautiously avoiding labelling the outing as a date.

Still, he couldn't help but lock eyes with her, searching for a flicker of interest.

Khynzy felt a rush of excitement, her heartbeat quickening. This invitation had a different texture to it, hinting at unspoken possibilities. "I'd love to," she responded, attempting to sound as casual as he had.

"Fantastic. Let's catch it, then," Levi said, doing his best to keep his voice steady. The anticipation was evident, hanging in the air long after their conversation ended.

Their cinematic journeys became explorative ventures, with thought-provoking films leading to intense debates and reflections. "The symbolism in that scene was striking," Levi would muse, and Khynzy would dive into the intricacies of the cinematography with fervour.

However, in the evenings, wearied by the strains of work, they'd opt for lighter, more straightforward films. Those nights were filled with easy laughs and unburdened gazes, a refreshing respite from their routine intellectual engagements.

"I appreciate the simple ones sometimes," Khynzy would say with a sigh of relief, her eyes relaxed. "Me too," Levi would agree, his posture eased. "Sometimes it's nice not to decipher every frame and just enjoy."

Their evolving narrative transcended the chosen films, becoming a harmonious dance of shared experiences and growing affection, a silent strengthening of bonds with each shared look and unwinding plot.

31

Unwanted Gift

Levi initially thought he was just like any other child. He believed everyone could hear the negative thoughts of others; that they simply didn't talk about it because it was considered a secret, something you're not supposed to talk about. He was eight when he discovered another unsettling gift amid the noise of the school cafeteria. **I'm going to steal that kid's lunch money,** a clear thought pierced through the clatter. The malicious intention came from a boy a few tables over who got up and walked toward a younger student.

Instinctively, Levi focused intently on the boy and thought, *Maybe you shouldn't; you might get caught.* Astonishingly, the boy hesitated, looked puzzled, and returned to his seat.

This uncanny ability—to pick up on people's harmful or negative thoughts and influence them—was a double-edged sword. While he could divert acts of cruelty or dishonesty, the emotional toll of knowing people's darker inclinations weighed heavily on him.

At home, later that night, the aroma of a home-cooked meal filled the air. Levi and his parents gathered around the dinner table. Despite the inviting smell of food, an invisible tension loomed like a storm cloud waiting to burst.

His mom thought about household bills and groceries: *Did I remember to pay the electricity bill? What if we can't afford groceries next week? If only I married someone more financially stable... What was I thinking? I love my family.* Meanwhile, his dad pondered a potential job opportunity: *Could I really take that job overseas? What would happen to my family? What if she falls for someone else while I'm away?*

"Dad, you're thinking about a job far away?" Levi suddenly blurted out.

Both parents froze. "What makes you say that?" his father cautiously inquired.

"I heard you think it," Levi simply replied.

His mother and father exchanged worried glances. "Levi, can you actually hear our thoughts?" his mom asked, her voice tinged with disbelief.

Before answering, his dad chimed in. "Let's test this out. I'll think of something, and you tell me what it is."

His father closed his eyes and thought of a happy day they had spent at the beach last summer. Levi squirmed in his chair, unable to say anything. His dad opened his eyes. "Well?"

"I didn't hear anything, Dad," Levi admitted.

His father's eyes narrowed slightly, filled with a mix of disappointment and concern. *Is he making this all up?*

Levi immediately spoke up, "No, Dad. I'm not making it up. You were just thinking whether I was lying or not."

His mother's eyes widened, and Levi could hear her next thought loud and clear: *What if people find out and try to take him away?*

"You're scared that someone will take me away if they find out," Levi whispered, looking at his mom.

His mother nodded, visibly concerned. "That's exactly what I'm scared of. We have to keep this a secret, okay?"

His father sighed deeply. "It seems he only picks up on our

worries or negative thoughts."

"I promise, I won't tell anyone," Levi assured them. "And Dad, if you want to work overseas, that's okay. We can be a family anywhere."

His father looked at him, eyes misty but grateful. "Thank you, Levi. That means everything to me."

After dinner, the family moved to the living room, each lost in their own thoughts. Levi's dad was still contemplating the overseas job, the weight of the decision hanging heavily: *If we move, will Levi adjust well? What about his schooling?*

Levi sent a thought to his dad, *Maybe it'll be fun, Dad. A new school could be cool.*

His dad perked up. "You know, moving for the job might not be such a bad idea. It could be a new adventure for all of us."

His mom looked puzzled. "You're suddenly optimistic. How come?"

"I don't know, the idea just came to me," his dad said, sharing a look with Levi.

His mom's thoughts shifted to a new realm of concern: *Can Levi influence thoughts now, too? That could be even more dangerous.*

"I heard that, Mom," Levi said softly, "but I promise to only use it for good stuff, like making people less worried."

His mom knelt down in front of him, locking eyes with her son. "Levi, these abilities of yours—they're special, but they could be misunderstood. We have to make some rules about when you can and can't use them, okay?"

His dad nodded, "Exactly. We have to protect this family."

"I promise to be careful," Levi reassured them, understanding the weight of his abilities more than ever.

Levi tried to fulfil this promise. But there were also times when Levi, in a bad mood or simply feeling the wear and tear of constantly hearing others' ill intentions, would suggest the opposite of the morally upright thing. "Go ahead, do it," he would think, an encouragement rather than a deterrent. In secondary school, when he did this during a basketball game, he heard a player from the opposing team think, "I could intentionally foul him and make it look accidental." Levi, frustrated and competitive, projected back, "Do it; you won't get caught." The player acted on it, and Levi's teammate, Owen, ended up injured. The guilt was immediate and gut-wrenching.

Levi soon understood the gravity of his choices. Every suggestion he made, good or bad, had consequences, and the moral landscape he navigated was treacherous.

In the days following the accident, Levi made it a point to visit Owen frequently, both at the hospital and then at his home. His guilt over what had happened drove him to be there as much as he could. During one of these visits, Owen, who possessed a more polished, typical heartthrob charm, in contrast to Levi's rugged attractive features, remarked with a hint of mischief in his tone, "What, you're here again? You into me or something?"

Levi, momentarily taken aback, responded by playfully tossing a pillow at Owen. "I don't swing that way," he shot back, half-annoyed, half-amused. This lighthearted exchange seemed to dispel some of the heaviness Levi felt. As he got up to leave, Owen's voice stopped him, softer this time. "Stay, please?"

Hesitating for a brief moment, Levi sat back down. Their camaraderie, now laced with shared jokes and understanding, evolved into a deeper friendship, moving beyond the guilt and misunderstandings of the past. This was the beginning of a strong and lasting bond between them.

As Levi matured, the ethical quandary he found himself in became increasingly complex. What right did he have to intervene in other people's thoughts? Yet, how could he not, knowing the potential harm or good he could do?

So he honed his skills, using them sparingly and only when he deemed it absolutely necessary. But the weight of his ability grew over time.

32

Rumors and Rings

Khynzy was at her desk, reviewing a design document, but her mind kept straying to Levi. She hadn't seen him in the office for a few days, which was unsettling. They usually left work together, or at least he'd drop by her desk if they couldn't have lunch together. The emptiness left by his absence weighed heavily on her.

Rather than approaching her desk as usual, Stella opted for a different route. She initiated a voice call via their office's online communication channel despite being in clear view of each other. Khynzy put on her headset and answered the call. Stella, a K-Drama fan, greeted her in Korean with an enthusiastic "Annyeonghaseyo!"

"You've been staring at that same page for a while now," Stella said, her voice tinged with concern. "Is everything okay?"

After hesitating briefly, Khynzy decided to confide in Stella. "I haven't seen Levi around, and it's bothering me."

Stella looked startled as if connecting some dots. "Oh! Are you two still dating? I had a feeling something was going on."

Taken aback, Khynzy nodded. "We're taking things slow, but yeah, something's happening."

Stella's fingers began to tap away on her keyboard. Moments later, a notification pinged from Khynzy's computer. She clicked the private chat window to find Stella's message: "You should know then, someone saw Levi and Rachel at a jewellery store. They were looking at engagement rings."

The room seemed to spin. Engagement rings? She and Levi hadn't even defined their relationship yet.

Stella looked concerned. "I thought you guys were serious. You've been spending a lot of time together."

"We are," Khynzy interjected softly, "or at least I thought we were. We wanted to take things slow, you know? This is unsettling."

Stella nodded sympathetically. "Talk to Levi, Khynzy. Clear the air."

Ending the call and closing the chat window, Khynzy attempted to refocus on her work, her thoughts churned with emotion. She knew she had to confront Levi, but apprehension clouded her heart.

When the workday was winding down, Khynzy decided she had to speak to Levi. She needed to know the truth. With a sense of purpose, she packed her things and headed to his desk.

What she saw when she arrived shook her. From a distance, she could see Levi and Rachel were engrossed in conversation, standing closer than Khynzy felt comfortable with. It was at this moment that Levi's ability kicked in. He heard Rachel's malicious thoughts clear as day: *Let's see how Khynzy likes seeing this.* Rachel laughed and touched his arm with what seemed like intimate familiarity. Realising Rachel was deliberately making it appear they were intimately close; he swiftly turned around to find Khynzy's eyes already on him. The confusion and hurt clouding her face struck him deeply.

Khynzy couldn't bear to watch any longer. She turned on her heel, heading swiftly away, her heart heavy and eyes stinging with unshed tears.

"Khynzy, wait!" Levi's voice trailed after her, tinged with desperation.

But she didn't wait. Hailing a cab, she climbed in, not looking back. Levi reached the curb just in time to see the cab pull away. His heart sank as he realised the extent of the misunderstanding.

Levi watched as her cab became a speck in the distance, his heart heavy. He knew he had a lot to clarify, and more importantly, he knew he couldn't let what they had just slip away without a fight.

While driving through the city, Khynzy felt a void open inside her, a mixture of confusion, hurt, and unspoken love.

33

A Knot Untangled

Khynzy stared at the screen of her security camera, her heart a chaotic mix of hurt and confusion. Levi stood outside, his posture one of earnest pleading. She wasn't ready to confront him—yet.

His voice came through the door, laced with a desperation she'd never heard from him before. "Khynzy, please open the door. You're misunderstanding the situation with Rachel. It's not what you think."

Hesitating, her hand trembling over the doorknob, she found her voice. "What about the jewellery store?"

Levi sighed, understanding her concern. "Rachel being there was pure coincidence. I was there for something entirely different. She spotted me and insisted on showing me her dream engagement ring. I didn't want to cause a scene or be impolite, so I humoured her for a moment."

Khynzy unlocked the door and opened it a sliver. She saw Levi's eyes, pools of sincerity and perhaps regret.

"I'm sorry, Levi," she said, her voice low, withholding the depth of her feelings. "I may have jumped to conclusions."

Relief crossed Levi's face. "I should've been clearer too. Can we talk about this?"

Khynzy nodded and let him in. Once inside, Levi reached into his pocket and took out a slim rectangular velvet case, handing it to her with a warm smile.

"Is this for me?" she asked, her voice tinged with cautious optimism.

"Yes," Levi replied, a soft smile on his face. "I bought it from the jewellery store the other day. I was planning to give it to you at a formal dinner to which I wanted to invite you, but given the circumstances, I thought now might be the right time."

Khynzy carefully opened the velvet case to reveal a delicate bracelet adorned with alternating diamonds and sapphires. An elegant 'L' charm added a personal touch. "It's breathtaking," she whispered.

Levi took the bracelet from the case and gently clasped it around Khynzy's wrist. "It looks even more beautiful on you," he said softly.

Just then, an audible growl from Levi's stomach broke the momentary tension. "I rushed here and skipped dinner," he admitted.

Khynzy moved to the kitchen and began preparing some pasta. The sizzle and aroma of the sauce filled the room. Levi, observing from a distance, couldn't help but be entranced by the smell.

"Zee, that smells so good," he said, using a nickname that held a certain intimacy.

Khynzy felt a warm flush of happiness at the nickname. Her parents and Aunt Mildred used to call her 'Zee-zee'. No one had ever called her 'Zee' before, and coming from Levi, it felt special—another intimate layer added to their deepening relationship.

As they sat down to eat, the room was filled with the comforting scent of the food and the sound of silverware against plates. The atmosphere was almost normal, but both knew that bigger conversations loomed on the horizon.

Clearing his throat, Levi finally broke the silence. "Zee, would you like to go to dinner with me this weekend? Just the two of us. It's a formal place, so you'll need to dress up," he added, emphasising the significance of the occasion.

Khynzy looked up from her plate, meeting his gaze. The formal invitation hung in the air between them, a clear acknowledgement from Levi that he wanted their relationship to move forward, even if neither was ready to fully disclose their feelings just yet.

After a moment, she smiled and nodded. "I'd love to, Levi. A formal dinner sounds wonderful."

34

Beneath the Moon and Sky Light

Levi had successfully snagged a reservation at one of the city's most exclusive rooftop restaurants, a venue so in demand that scoring a booking was akin to finding a single statement from a million lines of programming code. He knew this unique spot, complete with mesmerising glass domes that glittered under the night sky, making them appear like enchanted bubbles amidst the urban jungle, would be the ideal backdrop for the intimate evening he envisioned with Khynzy.

They found themselves inside one of the glass domes and sat side by side on a plush sofa perfect for two, enveloped in a world of their own. Twinkling fairy lights graced the railings, candles flickered on the tables like distant stars, and above them, the sky was a limitless canvas, its celestial wonders twinkling like diamonds.

As they waited for their meal, a palpable tension filled the air—sweet, anticipatory, charged. With his gaze fixed on the horizon, Levi subtly moved his hand closer to where Khynzy's hand lay on the sofa. His fingertips barely brushed against hers before pausing, giving her a moment to react. When she didn't pull away, a sense of relief washed over him.

Gently intertwining their fingers, he felt the warmth and softness of her hand envelop his own, sending a comforting wave of ease through him. Khynzy felt it too—a tingling sensation that seemed to climb up her arm, making her heart flutter. Levi lifted their conjoined hands to rest on his thigh. Levi couldn't help but notice the delicate bracelet he had gifted her the other night. The alternating diamonds and sapphires sparkled subtly, and the 'L' charm glinted, adding a personal touch to their shared moment. Simultaneously, his thumb began to caress the soft skin of her palm in a soothing, circular motion. This sent ripples of excitement coursing through them both, subtly amplifying the emotional resonance of the evening.

They enjoyed a quiet dinner, their conversation flowing as smoothly as the wine they sipped.

"Do you ever wonder what's out there?" Khynzy asked, setting down her glass and staring up at the sky.

Levi looked at her and then up at the celestial canvas overhead. "All the time. It's a constant motion up there."

She nodded, "Yes–planets orbit stars, stars move through galaxies, and maybe galaxies themselves drift in an unseen dance."

"But in all that motion," Levi turned his focus back to Khynzy, "I'm captivated by a single Skylyght right here." His voice, a mere whisper, mingled with the peaceful silence.

Khynzy's eyes met his, blushing at his words, her heart pounding in her chest. The atmosphere seemed to shift, growing thicker with tension and anticipation. Levi stood up, extending his hand toward her. "Would you like to get a better view?"

Hand in hand, they walked towards the dome's entrance. The city sprawled beneath them like a sea of glowing jewels, but it was the sky that caught their attention, an expansive dome dotted with stars.

Turning to face her, Levi's hands found their way to her waist, pulling her gently towards him. In response, Khynzy's hands rested gently on his chest, feeling the subtle yet reassuring rhythm of his heartbeat beneath her fingers. And for a few heartbeats, they just looked at each other as if asking for silent permission.

Levi leaned in, and the moment their lips touched, it was as if a circuit was completed, sending a surge of electricity through them both. The kiss was tender yet passionate, as if they were pouring all the unspoken feelings of the night into this one moment. Khynzy felt Levi's grip tighten around her waist as if he was anchoring himself to her and she to him.

They finally broke the kiss but remained close, foreheads touching, sharing the same air. Levi's heart raced as he whispered, "With you, McKhynzy Skylyght, I don't need to look at the sky to see the light." The delicate confession lingered softly in the space between them.

A gentle breeze caressed Khynzy's hair as she locked eyes with Levi, finding a universe of affection in his gaze. "And with you, Levi Echo Moonstrider," she whispered back, the faintest of smiles warming her words, "I don't need the moon to light up my nights."

It was as if time had paused, allowing them to delve deep into each other's souls. Even this simple act of locking eyes felt incredible, like finding a piece of themselves they didn't know was missing. It was a connection that went beyond physical touch, grounding them in the present moment and foreshadowing all the potential futures they could share. Then, as if guided by some invisible force, they leaned in for another kiss. This one was different—still filled with emotion, but also a newfound certainty, as if sealing a pact only the two of them understood.

The stars above twinkled brighter as though acknowledging the cosmic shift that had unfolded in their small, intimate universe. On that rooftop, at that moment, they knew they were at the start of something monumental, something neither could nor would ever walk away from.

35

It's Official

For a month following their romantic dinner date, Levi and Khynzy explored the uncharted territories of being an official couple.

During a virtual team meeting at the start of their first week, the opportunity arose for Levi to make their relationship official in a workplace setting. "Ah, it looks like we have a guest appearance in the background," Levi's manager chuckled as Khynzy walked past in the frame. Levi grinned and said, "Oh, you all know Khynzy. She's from the Code squad. We often collaborate on projects." He then pulled her gently toward the camera and added, "And on a more personal note, she's also my girlfriend."

There were a series of reactions—smiles, nods, and a few thumbs-up emojis flashed on the screen. Khynzy, blushing but delighted, leaned in and waved, saying, "Hi, everyone."

❦

Later that evening, Khynzy sat in her living room, excited but slightly nervous to share the news with her circle. Stella had already sent her a message, having gotten a tip from someone on Levi's team. "Spill the beans, girl!" it read. Khynzy couldn't help but smile as she dialled Stella's number for a video call.

"Hey, annyeong," Khynzy greeted.

"Annyeong yourself! So, are you going to keep me in suspense or what?" Stella retorted.

"Okay, okay," Khynzy laughed. "Levi and I are officially a couple. He also introduced me as his girlfriend during his team meeting today."

Stella squealed, "Finally! I knew you two were perfect for each other. How did it feel to be introduced as his girlfriend?"

"It was amazing, Stella. We've been in this limbo for so long, and to have it be so public and definite... it felt like a dream," Khynzy shared.

Stella nodded, her eyes glossy. "I'm so happy for you, Khynzy. Can't wait for a double date!"

"Let's make that happen," Khynzy agreed happily.

🍒

Meanwhile, at their favourite downtown bar, the click of pool balls echoed as Levi and Owen engaged in a friendly match. Though Levi was always a focused player, tonight, there was an extra twinkle in his eye. After sinking another ball, Owen remarked, "You're giving off a different vibe tonight. What's the deal?"

Levi hesitated for a moment, then said, "You remember Khynzy, right?"

Owen laughed, "The one you couldn't tear your eyes away from at the casino? The one you almost stood me up for? Been spending a lot of time with her, huh?"

Levi smirked, "Guilty as charged. She's my girlfriend now."

Owen raised an eyebrow, impressed. "Well, well, Mr. Smooth. When are you going to introduce your best friend to her?"

Levi laughed, "Soon, man. Promise. I think you two will get along perfectly."

🍒

Later that week, Levi and Khynzy nestled on Khynzy's couch for a movie marathon, a heap of gourmet popcorn between them. As the credits rolled on the last film, Levi pulled her close for a lingering kiss, sealing a perfect day.

Week two featured a culinary adventure, preparing shrimp and grits together in Levi's kitchen. "Garlic or no garlic?" Khynzy called out from her cooking station. "Always garlic," Levi replied as he chopped vegetables.

In the third week, they embarked on a triple date: Levi and Khynzy, Stella and her boyfriend Mark, and Owen with his girlfriend Samantha. Together, they tackled the challenges of an escape room adventure. The atmosphere was charged with excitement, especially when they unlocked the final door, signalling their victory.

Later, back at Levi's place, they celebrated their triumph by making homemade sushi rolls. A palpable warmth and camaraderie enveloped the room as they raised their glasses in a toast to friendship and their successful escape.

During the fourth week, Khynzy was under the weather. Levi arrived at her door with a care package featuring her favourite green tea, vitamin C, and a pair of cute, cuddly toys —a panda and a wolf. His attentive care won him a raspy "You're amazing" from Khynzy. Levi reciprocated this with a loving forehead kiss and whispered, "So are you."

As the month came to a close, they found themselves reflecting on their new relationship. Their hearts were full of love, their minds buzzing with future plans as they embraced the endless possibilities ahead, knowing they had something incredibly special in each other.

36

Harmonic Fusion

Khynzy's livestream was alive with anticipation. She had a surprise in store for her social media followers. She usually live-streamed her drum covers but had not collaborated with anyone before.

She glanced at the camera, her fingers drumming rhythmically on her thighs. She was perched on the drum stool, clad in her usual attire: a black mesh top with a sweetheart tube beneath and torn jeans—her PandaDrummer identity intact with the iconic brown paper bag featuring endearing panda eyes with fluffy black patches around the eyeholes. The chat was already buzzing. Fans and curious viewers had gathered for what was sure to be an unforgettable experience.

The door to the music room creaked open, and Levi entered, filled with anticipation. He also wore a brown bag over his face, but it was different. His was a mask of a wolf—a playful nod to his "WolfStrummer" alter ego. The masks added an element of mystery and magic to the scene.

"Hey there, Wolf Strummer," Khynzy greeted, her smile evident even beneath her paper bag.

Levi's grin was unmistakable behind the bag over his head

that hid his identity, his enthusiasm infectious. "Hey, Panda Drummer."

"Are you ready for this?" Khynzy asked, her eyes dancing.

Levi nodded, his fingers strumming the strings of his guitar in anticipation. "Absolutely. Let's give them something they won't forget."

As Khynzy settled onto her drum stool and Levi positioned himself nearby, the room seemed to hum with an electric energy. The chat continued to scroll with messages—waves of support, emojis, and anticipatory comments.

Khynzy started with a gentle drum roll, setting the rhythm for their performance. Levi's guitar strings responded, each note harmonising with the beat of the drums. The music swelled, weaving a tapestry of sound that was both powerful and enchanting.

As the song progressed, Khynzy's drumming became more intricate, mirroring Levi's skilful guitar work. Their music blended seamlessly, a harmonious fusion of rhythm and melody. They navigated the shifts and crescendos with an innate understanding, each note building upon the other to create something extraordinary.

And all the while, the chat was alive with reactions:

"WolfStrummer and PandaDrummer—a match made in music heaven!"

"The mystery behind the bags only adds to the magic of their collaboration!"

"I'm absolutely blown away by their talent and connection!"

As the final chords rang out, Khynzy and Levi exchanged triumphant looks. The energy in the room was palpable, an echo of the music that had just resonated through the walls. The applause from the virtual audience was thunderous, a testament to the impact their collaboration had made.

"Thank you all for joining us tonight," Khynzy said, her

voice filled with gratitude. "This was a special moment for us, and we're so glad we could share it with all of you."

Levi nodded in agreement. "Absolutely. Your support means the world to us."

As the live stream concluded, the screen was flooded with comments expressing awe and appreciation. The shared experience had not only showcased their musical talents, but had also deepened their connection. Their individual personas, represented by the masks, had merged into a singular force of creativity and emotion.

After a moment of silence, Khynzy stood up and approached Levi, her voice calm. "We did it, didn't we? We created something amazing together."

Levi grinned, his eyes sparkling behind the wolf mask. "Absolutely. It's like our music became one."

She chuckled softly. "You know, despite these bags, I feel like we understand each other."

Levi's gaze softened. "It's true. Our music speaks louder than any words could."

With a playful gleam in their eyes, they leaned in, their masked faces coming together in an attempt to kiss. But the bags got in the way, and they burst into laughter, the joy of the moment enveloping them.

As they removed their paper bags, anticipation hung in the air. Slowly, the bags came off, revealing their faces to each other.

And then, without hesitation, they leaned in again, their lips meeting in a sweet kiss—a culmination of their emotions, their music, and their deepening connection.

As they pulled away, their eyes met, and they shared a tender smile that spoke volumes. In that moment, as they stood face to face, their love felt stronger than ever.

37

Shared Corners

While they hadn't officially moved in together, Khynzy gradually became a fixture in Levi's apartment. The evidence of their deepening relationship could be found in subtle yet meaningful changes throughout their respective living spaces.

In Levi's home office, the most recent addition was a sleek table he had purchased specifically for Khynzy. It now stood adjacent to his desk, its surface neatly organised with Khynzy's essentials—a laptop covered in colourful stickers, her preferred ergonomic mouse, and a charming potted succulent. Levi was struck by how much warmer and more inviting his once-solitary workroom felt with her belongings in it.

Similarly, in Khynzy's apartment, Levi had also gained some real estate. His favourite running shoes were parked beside her collection of brogues and white sneakers, a stash of his preferred coffee blend took up space in her pantry, and a dedicated drawer had been cleared out for a handful of his essential clothing items—making impromptu sleepovers less cumbersome.

Both of them cherished their growing collection of framed

photographs. These snapshots on Levi's living room shelves captured everything from escape room adventures to jam sessions where Khynzy was on the drums, and Levi was rocking out on the guitar. Each photo was a visual chapter in their unfolding love story.

On one particular evening, Khynzy showed up with a package in hand. "I thought these would look perfect," she announced, unveiling a set of modern bedsheets that seamlessly integrated with Levi's room decor.

He laughed warmly. "Your sense of style is making my place look exponentially better."

As they made the bed with the new sheets, Khynzy paused, her hands running over the fabric to smooth out the last wrinkles. She looked up and found Levi's gaze already on her. His eyes glowed warmly, but what caught her attention was the absent hue of an aura around him. That enigma, the inexplicable invisibility of his aura, was a lingering curiosity —one of the small, unresolved mysteries that dotted the landscape of their love story. Yet, one thing was abundantly clear for all the unanswered questions: their lives were entwined in the most intricate ways, shaping a narrative that neither had anticipated, but both were eager to continue writing, one loving detail at a time.

Levi broke the comfortable silence, a grin forming on his face. "This really feels like home now, doesn't it, Zee?"

Hearing him say her name shortened intimately, she decided it was her turn to reciprocate. "It does, Lev," she said, using the shortened form of his name for the first time. The word felt right as it passed through her lips, like a soft-spoken affirmation of their growing intimacy.

Levi's eyes twinkled at the sound of his name being shortened for the first time by her. It was a small but meaningful shift, signalling that their relationship was taking on new layers of closeness.

At that moment, Khynzy felt her resolve strengthening. She had been contemplating when to share her unique ability to see auras. Levi—Lev, now—was shaping up to be someone she could trust with her deepest secrets.

38

The Colours of Trust

The evening had taken on a magical quality, the kind only found in the tranquil moments after a shared meal and heartfelt conversation. Deciding the atmosphere indoors was too confining for what she had to say, Khynzy suggested they step outside. They settled into the patio chairs, enveloped by the velvety darkness of the night sky, punctuated by stars.

Levi looked at Khynzy, waiting for her to speak, sensing the importance of what was about to be shared.

"Zee, what's on your mind? You look like you're about to tell me the secrets of the universe," he joked, lightening the mood.

She chuckled, but her eyes remained serious. "In a way, I am. Lev, you're the first person I'm telling this to, apart from my parents and my aunt. I can sense auras, colours that surround people and represent different emotions or traits."

Levi was stunned but intrigued. "That's incredible. So what does my aura look like?"

Khynzy met his gaze with a mixture of tenderness and regret. "That's the thing. I can't see your aura. It's as if you're a blank canvas. I've never experienced that with anyone else before."

Levi felt a strange mixture of disappointment and relief. Was it good or bad that he didn't have an aura? He wasn't sure, but it added another layer of complexity to their relationship.

"Could you give me an example? Like, can you see auras from here?" Levi asked, looking out into the neighbourhood.

"Sure," Khynzy nodded. She glanced at a couple walking down the street, their laughter in the air. "See that couple there? The man has a strong green aura, which often means he's compassionate and grounded. The woman has shades of blue and purple, indicating she's intuitive and peaceful."

Levi was fascinated, taking a moment to let this sink in. "Wow, that's really amazing. So you could read people's emotions before they even speak?"

"Yes, but it's not as simple as that. Auras can change based on mood, experiences, or even who someone is with. It's just a part of them, not their entirety."

"Do you remember that lift incident? I hesitated to step in because I saw the aura of the people inside the lift was inky black instead of the usual vibrant hues. Well, except for you; even on that day, I couldn't see your aura."

Levi nodded, absorbing this. While he wasn't ready to share his secret ability, the weight of holding it seemed lighter, knowing that Khynzy had trusted him with her unique gift.

He sat there, contemplating the depth of what Khynzy had just shared. Finally, he broke the silence with a question that popped into his mind. "Do animals have auras too? What about plants?"

Khynzy smiled, pleased by his curiosity. "Yes, they do. Animals have simpler auras, usually representing their most dominant emotional state. As for plants, their auras are even less complex, but they're there."

"That's incredible. I never thought of the world as being

so... colourful, in a literal sense," Levi mused. "What about the underwater world? Do fish and sea creatures have auras?"

She paused, her eyes sparkling as if delighted by his question. "I've never had the chance to see for myself, but I'd imagine they do. The ocean is a mysterious place, full of life and emotion. I'd love to explore it someday and see what colours lie beneath the surface."

Levi looked at her, captivated not just by her unique ability but also by the poetic way she described the world. He wondered how much more vivid and complex her world was compared to his own. Would he ever get the chance to share his ability with her, to make her see the world through his eyes, as she had just done for him?

As he sat there, pondering these thoughts, he realised he was falling even more deeply in love with Khynzy. She had just shared a part of her that was sacred and, in doing so, had made him feel a level of intimacy and connection that he had never felt before. He felt blessed to be a blank canvas in her colourful world and, for the first time in a long time, looked forward to painting a future full of colours together.

Levi grinned, recalling memories of seeing Khynzy at the casino. "Ah, so that's your secret weapon. I've seen you clean up at the casino; you're a real card shark."

Khynzy's eyes twinkled, and her smile widened. "Well, I can't deny that my ability gives me a slight edge. But you should know, most of my winnings go to charity."

That admission made Levi's admiration for her grow even stronger. "Even when you win, you find a way to make it about others."

Levi looked at her, his eyes full of affection. "You're truly amazing, Zee. Using your gift for something good like that... it makes me admire you even more."

For Levi, this felt like yet another perfect moment in a string of perfect moments, each one painting their future in increasingly vivid hues. With Khynzy by his side, he felt they could face whatever challenges lay ahead, turning them into something beautiful.

As the evening sky transformed into a palette of stars and fading sunlight, Levi felt a deeper connection forming between them. Knowing that Khynzy used her unique gift for the greater good only amplified his feelings for her. The thought of a future together seemed more appealing than ever, and he realised that with her, life would be an adventure filled with unexplored colours and untapped emotions.

39

Beneath the Surface

Levi had always been a man of surprises, and his next invitation was no exception. On a bright Thursday afternoon, with the promise of a sunny weekend ahead, he approached his girlfriend with an adventurous proposition.

"Zee," he began, a mischievous glint in his eyes, "how do you feel about scuba diving?"

Khynzy's eyes widened with excitement at the prospect. She had often wondered how auras would manifest underwater, and the idea of exploring the depths with Levi intrigued her. "Scuba diving? I've never done it before, but I'd love to try it!"

Levi's smile widened as he said, "Fantastic! There's a beautiful spot not too far from here. I'll arrange for a dive this weekend."

Khynzy hesitated for a moment, assuming it would be a group outing. However, she realised it was just the two of them when he added, "It's just you and me, a chance to experience something extraordinary together."

Her heart raced, a mix of anticipation and curiosity coursing through her. She agreed, her adventurous spirit taking hold. "I can't wait to see what underwater auras look like."

As the weekend approached, Khynzy found herself eagerly preparing for the dive. The thought of spending quality time with Levi filled her with a sense of anticipation.

On the day of the dive, they arrived at the dive site, suited up in wetsuits and gear. Khynzy couldn't help but wonder how the underwater world would reveal itself to her aura-seeing eyes. She adjusted her scuba gear with a mix of excitement and curiosity. Levi squeezed her hand reassuringly. He had arranged this underwater adventure after Khynzy had confided in him about her unique ability to see auras, not just of people but also of plants and animals.

As they descended into the depths, Khynzy's eyes widened in wonder. The marine world came alive in more colours than she had ever imagined. The coral reefs, teeming with marine life, emanated vibrant auras that danced and mingled with each other, creating an ethereal tapestry of energy.

A calming blue aura surrounded the majestic sea turtle that swam past them. Its eyes, deep and wise, seemed to acknowledge Khynzy's presence, making her wonder if it sensed her gift. Small fish, darting between the corals, left trails of golden and orange auras akin to fireflies weaving through a night sky.

Levi pointed towards a graceful spotted eagle ray, its aura a combination of whites and purples, symbolising its pure and regal nature. The sun's rays filtering through the water illuminated the scene, making the auras even more pronounced.

Khynzy, feeling an overwhelming connection to this underwater realm, turned to Levi, her eyes glistening. He smiled, understanding the depth of her experience. This dive was more than just an adventure; it was a profound journey into a world where Khynzy's gift was a bridge between the seen and the unseen.

As Khynzy and Levi continued their exploration, they ventured into an area of the reef that looked like a vibrant underwater garden. Pops of pink and white coral structures stood tall, resembling otherworldly trees and bushes against the cerulean backdrop. Swirls of smaller fish moved in harmonious schools, their colours blending seamlessly with the surroundings.

Khynzy couldn't help but be drawn into the intricate dance of life underwater. She noticed that the auras of the fish would shift and change as they interacted with each other. When predators approached, the auras of the prey would pulsate with anxiety and fear, creating a visual symphony of emotion.

Among the marine life, a pair of clownfish caught Khynzy's attention. These playful fish danced around a large, translucent anemone, its tentacles swaying gently with the water's current. With their striking orange and white patterns, the clownfish seemed to be playing a game of hide-and-seek, darting in and out of their protective anemone home. Their auras were bright and triumphant, a mix of radiant yellows that mirrored their cheerful disposition.

The contrasting colours of the reef, from the deep reds of the soft corals to the muted greens and browns of the stony corals, painted a surreal and enchanting picture. Khynzy felt like she had entered a fairy tale where every creature had its own story. The soft glow of their auras, each unique in colour and intensity, added to the magic of the moment.

Levi, who had organised this intimate adventure, watched Khynzy with a newfound appreciation. Her ability to perceive the beauty of the underwater world in such a unique way fascinated him. Observing Khynzy's enchantment, he pulled her close, their bubbles mingling as they shared a silent, underwater embrace. The world above seemed distant as they revelled in the wonder of the deep, connected not just by their relationship, but by the shared experience of nature's unparalleled beauty.

Their scuba diving expedition provided a glimpse into the hidden world beneath the waves and deepened the connection between Levi and Khynzy. It was a journey into uncharted waters, where every shimmering aura told a story of life, beauty, and the mysteries of the ocean.

40

The Gift of Time

Seated in the tucked-away corner of the Italian restaurant they loved so much, Levi and Khynzy felt uniquely at ease. This hidden gem within the restaurant served as a sanctuary for both of them. For Khynzy, who saw auras emanating from everyone else, it was the one place where her vision wasn't crowded with hues—especially because Levi's aura remained a mystery to her. Likewise, Levi, who could usually hear the swirl of people's thoughts, found comfort here; in particular, Khynzy's mind was a space he couldn't penetrate, a welcome respite from the negative thoughts of others.

Levi was dressed in a tailored navy suit that brought out the depth in his eyes. He kept stealing glances at Khynzy, who was equally stunning in a sapphire blue dress that highlighted her features, her subtle silver earrings catching the soft glow of the candlelight, adding just the right touch.

Khynzy, in turn, found herself enchanted by how Levi looked in his suit, as though it were custom-made just for him, much like the unique bond they shared. She felt almost dreamy, as if floating in a surreal bubble, unable to fully grasp that this incredible man was hers.

The air was perfumed by the inviting aromas of garlic and

a hint of fresh herbs. A violinist played at a distance, far enough not to intrude but close enough for their melodies to be heard. The music seemed to capture the essence of their unique love story. Surrounded by this blend of sensory experiences and illuminated by the soft candlelight, they seemed to exist in a world all their own, affirming the special bond they shared.

"As always, Marco outdid himself," Levi said, referring to the chef, who was also a long-time friend. "I'll have to swing by the kitchen later and thank him."

"The porcini is amazing," Khynzy agreed. "You're lucky to have a friend who's such a culinary genius."

Both were keenly aware that tonight was no ordinary outing; it was a dual celebration. Remarkably, their birthdays fell on the same day, albeit two years apart, a coincidence that seemed almost fated.

"So, should we do gifts now or after dessert?" Khynzy asked, her eyes twinkling with anticipation.

"Let's do it now. I can't wait any longer," Levi responded, almost too eagerly.

Khynzy produced a small, tastefully wrapped box from under her chair and slid it across the table to him. "For you, my Lev," she said, the phrase echoing in the air, sounding almost like "my love," as if she'd woven both his name and her affection into a single, intimate expression.

Levi looked up, catching her gaze as he felt the weight of the small box in his hands. His eyes shimmered, clearly touched by the nuance in her words. At that moment, he felt an overwhelming sense of closeness.

He carefully unwrapped the box, lifting its lid to reveal an exquisite watch cushioned on plush velvet. The watch's face was a mesmerising deep blue, framed by a silver bezel that gleamed in the soft candlelight. Its hands and hour markers were luminescent, softly glowing like far-off stars. Adding an elegant, masculine touch was a finely crafted steel bracelet that seemed to mesh seamlessly with the overall design. This wasn't just a watch; it was a masterpiece of craftsmanship.

"Wow, this is absolutely stunning," Levi exclaimed, unable to peel his eyes away from the intricate details. "I can't believe you did this."

A playful grin spread across Khynzy's lips. "Let's just say I diverted some of my poker winnings into an investment that's always on time."

Levi laughed, slipping the watch onto his wrist. It felt like a perfect fit, both literally and metaphorically. "You know, I've always had a soft spot for traditional watches. There's a history and craftsmanship that you just can't get with smartwatches. This is truly special, Zee."

Her eyes shone brighter, thrilled by his heartfelt reaction. Levi reached under his chair and brought out a petite, ornately wrapped box. "Now, it's your turn."

Heart pounding in her chest, Khynzy unwrapped the gift. As she opened the box, her eyes widened in sheer astonishment. It was a watch, and not just any watch—this was the women's counterpart to the one she had gifted Levi. The silver bezel was adorned with tiny, sparkling gems that caught the candlelight, and the face exhibited the same mesmerising blue hue. Completing this work of art was a delicately crafted steel bracelet mirroring Levi's but with a feminine touch.

She looked up, "You've got to be kidding me," she laughed in disbelief, "This is too perfect. We got each other matching watches?"

Levi chuckled, equally stunned, "I guess great minds think alike, or in this case, great hearts."

Khynzy playfully adjusted the watch around Levi's wrist and clicked it into place. "There you go. As if you needed another reason to look dashing."

Levi laughed softly, taking her wrist in his hands. He fastened her watch with equal care, its matching steel bracelet glinting in the candlelight. "Guess we're both levelling up our style game, huh?"

Their eyes met, and in that moment, both couldn't help but marvel at how perfectly the watches—and they themselves—fit together.

"And speaking of perfect moments," Levi said softly, leaning in, "this feels like one."

He kissed her, a kiss filled with sweetness and a passion that made the rest of the world recede into the background. When they pulled away, their eyes locked once again, mirroring the same emotional depth.

"Here's to a lifetime of perfect moments," Khynzy whispered, her voice tinged with emotion.

Levi grinned, "And to never missing a single one."

They clinked their wine glasses together, a ceremonial gesture that sealed the promise held within each tick of their new watches—a tangible reminder of the irreplaceable, ever-flowing gift of time they intended to share, now and forever.

41

A Night To Remember

The company's Christmas ball was a dazzling affair held at an opulent hotel hall. Crystal chandeliers, gilded accents, and a live orchestra set the scene. Everyone was dressed to the nines.

Levi was a vision in his tailored black tuxedo, a crisp white shirt, and matching bow tie. His eyes, however, were solely focused on Khynzy. She was breathtaking in her teal gown, a masterpiece that seemed designed just for her. It clung perfectly to her curves and flowed gracefully down to the floor, its plunging neckline and delicate straps adding the right touch of allure. The dress accentuated all her best features, elegant but not flashy.

Despite the crowd, Khynzy and Levi felt enveloped in their own private bubble. Still, Khynzy couldn't help but notice the auras of other women in the room subtly shift when Levi walked by; vibrant hues of fuchsia or excited yellows would flash momentarily, only to be replaced by shades of greenish envy as they realised he was with her.

"You look amazing, Khynzy," Rachel from Levi's team remarked, her aura betraying a brief flare of envy.

"Thank you, Rachel. You look beautiful, too," Khynzy

replied with a genuine smile.

As they moved through the crowd, Khynzy caught a whiff of Levi's scent. It was subtle but distinctly him—a mixture of cologne and his natural aroma that she found incredibly alluring. She's struck not just by his scent but also by his overall presence - the way he looked in his tailored tuxedo, the confidence with which he moved. His aura was one she couldn't see, but his presence was radiating an energy that was irresistibly captivating.

Across the room, Levi sensed an array of thoughts from the men, who couldn't help but appreciate how stunning Khynzy looked. Levi had to endure the unsolicited fantasies that played out in the minds of other men in the room— disrespectful thoughts about Khynzy that seemed almost blasphemous, given how deeply he cared for her. He even caught a few thoughts wishing he wasn't in the picture, fuelling his desire to be closer to her.

Wow, look at her, she's stunning... If only Levi wasn't in the picture, thought Leo, a colleague from the finance department. His thoughts were tinged with a lustful yearning that made Levi's skin crawl.

Another, a visiting client, even went as far as to fantasise about dancing with Khynzy himself. *She's hot! Levi doesn't deserve her*, he arrogantly thought.

Levi's grip on Khynzy's hand tightened imperceptibly as he felt another intrusive thought slither into his awareness. He was reminded once again that she was the exception, the one person whose thoughts he couldn't hear, which made him want to understand her even more.

Khynzy was equally enamoured. She found herself increasingly drawn to him as the evening wore on. It wasn't just her favourite scent of him; it was the whole package - the twinkle in his eyes, the laughter that seemed only for her, and the way he carried himself, an unspoken assurance that she found incredibly alluring.

After one last dance, he leaned in to whisper, "Shall we go?" The electric charge between them was unmistakable.

Meeting his gaze, Khynzy replied softly, "Yes," a word now imbued with layers of unspoken promises.

As they threaded through the crowd, every step away from the ballroom felt like a step toward liberation. It wasn't just a room they were leaving; it was a cacophony, a labyrinth of desires and judgments, not their own. And every step toward the exit was a step toward a world where the only thoughts he would somehow sense would be the one that belonged to the woman walking beside him.

The ride back to his apartment was a silent journey filled with thrilling anticipation. As the lift doors slid open, the quiet hallway that led to Levi's apartment was revealed. The tension between them was palpable, an electric current that neither could ignore. As they walked, Khynzy's teal dress shimmered under the soft lighting, her scent mingling with Levi's, creating an intoxicating blend that seemed to draw them closer together.

Unlocking the door, Levi allowed Khynzy to enter first. Her eyes caught sight of a framed photo on a shelf, a happy moment frozen in time.

As Levi closed the door behind them, Khynzy turned to face him, their eyes meeting in a silent acknowledgement of the emotion that had been building all evening. The magnetism between them reached a breaking point, and Levi closed the gap, capturing her lips in a gentle and insistent kiss. Khynzy felt her heart race as Levi's hands found their way to her waist, pulling her closer. The passionate kiss left them both breathless.

Breaking away just enough to look into her eyes, Levi said softly but earnestly, "I want you."

The room seemed to hold its breath, awaiting her response.

Finally, with a look of longing and affection, Khynzy replied, "I want you too."

In that instant, any remaining barriers between them crumbled.

Unable to wait any longer, Levi led her into his bedroom. Their clothes, so meticulously chosen for the Christmas ball, lay forgotten on the floor. What remained was the profound connection between them, now laid bare in its most intimate form.

Surrendering to the embrace of the night, the world outside ceased to exist. In its place arose a closeness that was indescribable yet profoundly felt. And in the quiet moments that followed, wrapped in each other's arms, they found a sanctuary that transcended the chaos of the world outside.

As they drifted into sleep, it was clear that something monumental had shifted. Their love had crossed a threshold, solidifying a commitment that was as extraordinary as it was profound.

42

A Light That Changes Everything

Khynzy and Levi strolled down the mall street, taking in the various storefronts. As they passed by a shop filled with luxurious chandeliers, Khynzy's eyes sparkled. "So pretty," she murmured.

"Why don't we take a closer look?" Levi suggested.

As they stepped into the shop, Levi's ears filled with the thoughts of those around him—a drawback of his unique ability. He could hear the cashier think, *More window shoppers. Why do people bother coming in if they can't afford any of this?* A passing couple's thoughts were even more disheartening. *Look at them, all lovey-dovey. They'll probably break up soon, just like everyone else.*

Khynzy, perceptive in her own way, noticed the cashier's aura—a dull grey tinged with streaks of green, signalling scepticism mixed with a tinge of envy.

As they browsed the shop, one chandelier caught Khynzy's eye. It was neither grandiose nor minimalistic but struck a balanced note of elegance and sophistication. The chandelier featured a few gracefully curved arms extending from a central hub. Each arm culminated in a clear crystal teardrop, delicately refracting the light. Made entirely of finely cut crystal, its radiance filled the room with a soft, inviting glow. Though not overly elaborate, its thoughtful design and careful craftsmanship made it a standout piece that Khynzy knew would be the perfect addition to Levi's living room.

Levi's thoughts were pulled back by Khynzy's excited voice, "Lev, look at this one! You should definitely get it for your living room. It would change the whole vibe, make it look so posh."

"Would you consider moving in with me if I get it?" Levi asked, a playful smile on his face.

Khynzy grinned, "Maybe."

The decision was made. Levi purchased the chandelier, ignoring the cashier's now shocked and slightly embarrassed thoughts.

❧

An hour later, they were back at Levi's apartment, unboxing the chandelier. Khynzy handed him tools and offered moral support as he wrestled with wires and fixtures. Finally, after a few tense minutes, Levi secured the last bolt.

Switching on the light, the room was transformed. The soft glow caught every surface, casting shadows that seemed to dance in celebration.

Khynzy stared up at the chandelier, utterly enchanted. "It changes the whole mood, doesn't it?"

Levi agreed but said nothing. Instead, he quickly tidied up, putting the tools and ladder back in their place, before heading to the kitchen. Khynzy sat cross-legged on the couch, her eyes glowing with affection as she watched Levi fumble in the kitchen. After 11 months together, Khynzy had shared her unique gift of seeing auras, though strangely, she couldn't see Levi's.

Levi's return to the living room was accompanied by two cups of steaming tea, the aroma intertwining with the air around them. "Zee, I have something of great importance to discuss with you," he voiced, his hands carefully placing the cups on the coffee table.

A wave of nervous curiosity wrapped around Khynzy's heart, causing it to flutter. *Is this the moment he asks me to move in?* Her thoughts danced around the possibility. The notion of sharing spaces, of waking up to shared mornings and experiencing the comforting presence of each other was tantalising. A silent affirmation resided in her heart, ready to be voiced.

Nervous but curious, she nodded. "Go ahead."

Her mind raced, painting pictures of a shared future. As she waited for his words, the glow from the chandelier above cast a warm light on the unfolding scene below.

"There's something about me that only my parents know," Levi began, his voice tinged with a hint of apprehension. "I can hear people's thoughts—specifically, the dark or negative ones. And sometimes, I can whisper back, nudging them toward better choices," Levi confessed.

"Do you hear mine?" Khynzy asked.

"No, you're the exception. I've never heard your thoughts," Levi replied. "I usually try not to invade the privacy of people I care about, not that I can turn it off, but you've always been an exception, even before I knew you."

"So, Owen doesn't know about this?" she sought confirmation, referencing Levi's best friend. "Considering how close you two are?"

Levi shook his head, a solemn expression crossing his face. "No, he doesn't. My parents' concerns made me cautious about sharing this with anyone, even Owen."

"I wonder why we're each other's exception?" Khynzy mused, her gaze thoughtful.

"I wish I knew. I can only tune in to negative thoughts, so maybe you've never harboured one in my presence?" he speculated.

Levi revisited the memory of their first encounter. "Do you

recall the lift accident? A man there had sinister plans to sabotage the train service. I intervened mentally, convincing him to abandon his malicious intent. Sadly, the explosive he carried detonated prematurely."

With eyes widened, Khynzy pressed, "So you use this gift to help people?"

"I try, but there have been times when I exploited it for personal benefit. It's not something I'm proud of," he admitted, his gaze dropping. "And I have one regret that haunts me the most..."

43

The Threads of Fate

Just a few weeks away from the milestone of becoming a teenager, Levi navigated the crowded airport; his dark hoodie pulled tightly over his head. Earbuds blared music into his ears, a futile barrier against the penetrating thoughts of strangers.

God, I hate my job. I should just quit.

Maybe I should leave him. He won't even notice I'm gone.

Look at that keychain. It would be so easy to just... take it.

Frustration brewed within Levi. His family had been bumped off their flight due to overbooking. The airline offered vouchers and apologies, hastily rebooking them on a flight set to depart in eight hours. As the reality sank in, Levi couldn't help but feel the day's plans slipping away, wasted. His parents, overwhelmed and stressed, tried to hide their disappointment.

Distracted by his own emotions, Levi found it challenging to carry out his usual, albeit secret, role: gently whispering into the minds of people grappling with negative or dangerous thoughts, subtly urging them towards better choices. Today, he had neither the focus nor the inclination.

Suddenly, a dark and ominous intention cut through the

mental fog, capturing Levi's full attention: *This plane won't reach its destination, and they'll all realise they were wrong to ignore me.* Levi zeroed in on the source, finding a man in his forties among the airport crowd, not an employee, but a passenger who had no intention of boarding the plane.

His thoughts were a volatile mix of anger and a twisted sense of justice. *They dismissed my findings, but after today, they won't be able to ignore the flaws in the system anymore.* Levi pieced it together; the man seemed to have manipulated the plane's software through his laptop, exploiting a vulnerability only he knew about.

Levi felt his stomach tighten. This was serious. Still burdened by his frustrations, he managed a mental plea: *Consider the consequences. Think about all the lives. Stop this now before it's too late.*

The man paused and hesitated momentarily as if grappling with an internal struggle. Then, with a determined look, he turned toward the waiting area. Levi lost his mental connection, the man moving out of his range of influence.

An hour later, Levi sat immobilised in front of the airport's public TV. The plane he and his family were supposed to be on had exploded mid-air. No survivors. A scrolling list of the deceased felt like a roll call of his own failures. His eyes were glued to the screen, unable to look away or escape the magnitude of his guilt.

A week passed, and Levi's eyes caught a news segment featuring the grieving families left in the wake of the disaster. One face caught his attention: a young girl about his age. Her eyes, red and swollen, were almost pleading through the screen as she spoke of the incomprehensible loss of her parents.

Can I fix this? Should I have done more? The questions churned in his mind, each one amplifying his guilt.

He was painfully aware of his limitations. While he could

hear and subtly influence thoughts, he could not bend people's will. Strangers suffering because of his missed opportunity faced a long, agonising journey towards healing. A journey Levi had no influence over.

He had been spared from the flight due to mere overbooking, a stroke of luck that now tasted bitterly ironic. His family was safe, but the weight of his inaction pressed down on him, a constant reminder of the lives he failed to save.

In his attempt to be a guardian angel, Levi had become a harbinger of doom—a burden he was now forced to bear for the rest of his life.

44

The Revelation

Levi recounted the airport story—the overbooked flight, his frustration, the man with the dark intention, and the ensuing crash.

Levi's revelations hit Khynzy like a bucket of ice water poured over her head. It was a sharp, piercing shock, a sudden jolt, making her shiver uncontrollably, her surroundings seeming to blur and dissolve. The chilling realisation consumed every thought, leaving her disoriented, her heart pounding in her chest. "Wait," she managed to utter in a shaky whisper, "that was the flight... the one my parents were on. They... that... that's how they died."

Levi's face was a picture of horror. "Oh God, Zee, I had no idea."

"You could have done something more? They might... they could still be walking around, breathing?" Her words were sharp, filled with a sense of betrayal and disbelief, slicing through the thick silence, showing all the raw pain she felt.

"I was... I was young, I was distracted... I was careless," Levi admitted, every word feeling like a heavy burden in his heart, his eyes swimming with regret. "I have to live with this, with the knowledge of this horrible mistake, every single day."

"My parents might still be alive, might still be with me, if you'd just tried a bit harder?!" Khynzy's words were harsh, cutting through the air, every syllable a direct hit of blame to Levi.

"I know, and I'm living with this guilt. I'll never forgive myself for it," Levi choked out, his whole being filled with remorse.

Khynzy, suddenly standing, her grip trembling around her bag, felt the whirlwind of her emotions spiralling out of control. Her breaths came in ragged, sharp intakes, her chest constricting as if bound by invisible cords. "I need... some time... to process this... it's too much." Her words were punctuated by gasps.

Levi, filled with regret and uncertainty, watched her, his heart in shackles. "Zee... I understand... Take your time... I'll be here, waiting... ready to talk, ready to... to be whatever you need." Quickly, before she could fully retreat, he wrapped her in a tight hug from behind, his body a silent manifestation of his apologies, his regrets.

"But... you're not... you're not... breaking up with me, right?" His whisper was fragile, his voice the ghost of his usual confidence.

"I... I... don't... know," she managed between sobs and hitched breaths, her voice fragmenting. Her tears cascaded freely, and the tremors rocking her body were palpable in the silence between them, filled with the echoes of untold pain.

Their embrace was a dance of regret and love, a moment frozen in the streams of their intertwined destinies. Her breaths became more erratic; each inhale a shallow gasp, the air seemingly thinning around her. The room seemed to spin as a wave of nausea entwined with the tightening sensation in her chest, her heart pounding irregularly, each beat a drum of chaos in her ribcage.

Levi, his face white with concern, watched as Khynzy's body trembled, her eyes clouded with pain and fear. "Zee, you can't breathe properly. I need to call an ambulance, or I can drive you to the hospital," he said, his voice laced with urgent worry.

Khynzy, her mind in turmoil, her lungs clawing for air, shook her head weakly, her voice barely above a whisper, strained and broken, "No."

Levi, his worry deepening, feeling helpless as he watched her struggle, made a quick decision. "At least let me call Stella."

Panic painting his features, he hastily dialled Stella's number. "Emergency," his voice was laced with palpable distress, "Khynzy's having an anxiety attack here at my apartment. She needs you urgently."

Fortune seemed to be on their side as Stella and her boyfriend, Mark, were nearby. They rushed to the apartment, arriving in a matter of minutes. Stella's face was a mask of worry as she embraced her struggling friend while Mark and Levi looked on, faces etched with concern.

Stella's eyes met Levi's, her gaze sharp, a silent accusation of 'What did you do?' flashing in them. Levi, his face a mix of guilt and worry, unable to meet her stare, shifted uncomfortably under her intense scrutiny.

Mark has bonded and is now friends with Levi. But as Stella's boyfriend and Khynzy, Stella's best friend, he is aligned with Khynzy by default.

Sensing the guilt emanating from Levi, Mark's thoughts begin to lace with anger and protectiveness. It pierced through Levi's consciousness, *Should I punch this guy?*, Mark's hand slowly curled into a tight fist at his side, a physical manifestation of his simmering rage. Even if Levi couldn't hear other people's negative thoughts, Mark's thoughts were loud in silent tension, unspoken but clearly vocalised by the anger flashing in his eyes.

"The hell did you do?!" Mark's voice resonated through the tense air, echoing the silent accusations swirling around the room.

Levi, his throat tight, words stuck, could only look at Mark, the weight of guilt anchoring him into silence, his gaze shadowed with regret.

Stella, her arm wrapped protectively around Khynzy, directed a final pointed look at Levi before turning to Mark. "Mark, we're leaving. Now." Her voice was firm, the undercurrent of anger unmistakable as she ushered a still-shaken Khynzy out of the apartment.

As they walked out, Khynzy's steps echoed with finality. Levi was left alone, rooted to the spot, his heart sinking into a silence that screamed with unspoken thoughts, unforgiven regrets, and a love that now seemed irrevocably lost.

Unsteady with emotion, his hand reached into his pocket and withdrew a small jewellery box. This was the day he had intended to propose, the reason he had finally revealed his extraordinary ability to hear thoughts - hoping to start their future with no secrets.

Slowly, he opened the box, revealing the ring he had chosen with hope and love. The sight of the delicate band and the glinting stone was a stark contrast to the fragments of his plans now lying in ruins. The ring, once a symbol of promise and connection, now looked back at him as a poignant emblem of what might never be.

45

Diverging Paths

Khynzy hesitated at her development manager's office door, her finger poised above the elegant wood. With a soft sigh, she tapped lightly, her heart fluttering in a peculiar dance of anxiety and relief. The dense aura around her seemed particularly vibrant today, a kaleidoscope of emotions that bled into the ether, invisible to all but her.

"Come in," called a mellow voice from within.

Khynzy stepped inside, clutching the crumpled envelope tightly in her trembling hand. She found Mr. Lewis sitting behind his desk, a gentle smile softening the lines of his concerned face. His aura gleamed a soothing blue, interwoven with streaks of earnest grey.

"Khynzy, please, take a seat. I've read your email..." He paused, studying her with a furrowed brow. Khynzy felt his aura flicker with a blend of disappointment and confusion.

She gently placed the envelope, her letter of resignation, back on his desk, her voice barely above a whisper. "I need to leave, Mr. Lewis."

He leaned back, his eyes still locked on hers, searching for answers in the pools of her tear-stained eyes. "I can't pretend I understand, Khynzy. You're among our best developers, and you've barely scratched the surface of your potential here."

Khynzy's gaze lowered, her voice breaking slightly. "It's... personal."

Mr. Lewis's aura fluttered with a sharp pinch of concern, turning a deeper shade of blue. "Has someone done something to make you feel uncomfortable here? Are you being harassed, Khynzy?"

She shook her head, pausing to gather the shattered remains of her composure. "No, nothing like that. It's just... my ex... he works here too. He's from a different squad, but... It's too hard to..."

Understanding flashed across Mr. Lewis's eyes, his aura morphing into a gentle lilac - empathy.

Mr. Lewis, absorbing the weight of her words and her pain, gently pushed the letter back towards her. "Khynzy," he began softly, "losing you would be a significant loss for our team. But I understand how hard this must be for you."

He hesitated before suggesting, "What if there was a way for you to stay with the company but put some distance between you and the personal issues? We have an overseas branch, Khynzy. It could be a fresh start."

Khynzy blinked, her mind swirling with the unexpected proposition. Her aura flickered with a myriad of colours, reflecting the chaos within. Could she leave everything behind? Was it an escape or a path to healing?

Mr. Lewis leaned forward, interlocking his fingers and placing them atop the dark oak desk. He looked at Khynzy, his aura splashing gentle waves of purple and blue across her perception, illuminating the sincerity embedded in his words.

"Khynzy, your skills, dedication, and innovative approaches have not only been recognised but have also become pivotal to our team," he began, his voice steady and comforting. "Your performance has been exemplary, and with the evaluations just around the corner, I was actually going to discuss your substantial raise and possible promotion."

Khynzy's eyes widened slightly, a delicate mix of surprise and appreciation reflected in her aura. Mr. Lewis continued, understanding the weight his words held.

"But it's not just about the numbers, is it?" He sighed softly. "I've seen how passionate you are about your work, Khynzy. And I believe—no, I know—that the issues you're facing are deeply personal and entirely valid."

He paused, leaning back, his aura subtly shifting to a soft green of gentle encouragement. "I won't pressure you, Khynzy. But I want you to consider the offer to move to the overseas branch. Think about it not as running away but as an opportunity for a fresh start. And yes, the raise and the potential promotion will follow you there. You've earned it. Your work speaks volumes about your capabilities."

Khynzy absorbed his words, the vibrant hues of her aura swirling with contemplation and uncertainty. Her mind raced with thoughts and what-ifs, battling between the familiarity of pain and the unfamiliarity of a new beginning.

"I... I need some time to think about it, Mr. Lewis," she replied after a brief pause, her voice softly intertwined with vulnerability and strength.

He nodded, his aura gently embracing the emotional turbulence in the room with understanding. "Take all the time you need, Khynzy. Just know that whatever decision you make will be respected and honoured here."

Khynzy stepped out of the office and stared at the door she had just closed, her mind whirling with emotions and reflections. A fresh start, a substantial raise, and a distance from the heartache that lingered in every corridor of the current office. The offer echoed in her thoughts, mingling with the soft hues of Mr. Lewis' empathetic aura that still lingered in her perception.

She turned back abruptly, reopening the door. Mr. Lewis,

who had just started to delve into another task, lifted his eyes, his aura pulsating with a mellow, welcoming glow.

"Mr. Lewis," Khynzy began, her voice trembling yet decisive, "how soon could the transfer be processed if I agree to it?"

He considered her for a moment, then spoke with an assuring calmness, "Khynzy, if you decide to proceed with this, I can expedite the transfer. It might take a week to process all the necessary paperwork and coordinate with the overseas branch. During that time, you could work from home—away from whatever memories or individuals might cause you distress here."

Her eyes, glossed with a sheen of unshed tears, met his. Khynzy could see in his aura a genuine want to help her navigate through the rocky terrains of her current predicament. A sincerity reached through her apprehension, providing a semblance of comfort in a world that had recently felt so cold and uninviting.

With a deep breath, she nodded. "Let's do it. I'll take the transfer."

Mr. Lewis's aura sparkled with various shades, reflecting relief, contentment, and a gentle excitement for Khynzy's new journey. "Very well," he agreed. "I'll get things moving immediately."

Khynzy lifted her eyes, vulnerability and gratitude mingling in her gaze. "Mr. Lewis, I can't thank you enough for understanding and supporting me through this."

His eyes softened, emanating warmth and comfort. "Khynzy," he assured, "I hope this move becomes a healing path for you. And always remember, if you ever wish to return, there will always be a place for you here."

As she stepped away from the office, this time, Khynzy's aura intertwined with a newfound resolve and a glimmer of hope, signifying the dawn of a new chapter that awaited her in an unfamiliar land.

46

Distance and Decisions

For a whole week, Khynzy had practically lived inside her apartment. As she transferred to a new squad, she navigated her days through the virtual corridors of her workplace, hiding behind emails, conference calls, and online meetings. Deep down, she felt numb and distant, as if she'd wrapped herself in a cocoon of solitude. It was as if she was adrift in a digital ocean, anchored only by her grief and decisions.

Levi, conversely, felt like he was sinking. Khynzy's absence had left a gaping void, a relentless tug that dulled the lights, muted the colours, and drained the joy from his everyday life. His mornings were the hardest, walking into an office devoid of her radiant smile, her presence. The empty chair at her desk became a daily indictment, a constant reminder of the chasm he had unwittingly carved between them.

In the initial days following their breakup, Levi restrained himself, giving the space Khynzy might have needed to think and heal. But as the evenings passed, his resolve waned under the weight of worry and longing. Reluctantly, after a week had passed, he found himself outside her apartment after work, his heart drumming in his ears. But it seemed the apartment was empty, and each unanswered knock bore into him, anchoring a deep, sinking feeling of despair and helplessness in his chest.

The next day, after what felt like an eternity of internal debate, Levi sought out Stella. As Khynzy's best friend and a key member of her work team, Stella was the likely gatekeeper of her secrets. If there were any hope of gaining insight into Khynzy's thoughts, Stella would be the one to provide it.

Finally mustering the courage, Levi approached Stella's cubicle and softly knocked on the partition. "Stella, do you have a moment?"

Stella looked up from her screen, her eyes reflecting a cautious curiosity. "Sure, what's going on?"

"It's about Khynzy."

Stella stood up and motioned for Levi to follow her. "Let's step into the small meeting room for a quick chat, just around the corner."

"Do you know where she is? She's been working from home for more than a week." Levi blurted out as soon as Stella closed the meeting room door intended for 1:1 catch-ups.

Levi's brows furrowed as he continued, his worry evident in his voice, "Actually, I'm not even sure she's at her apartment. I've tried visiting, but it seems empty every time. The lights are always out, and she hasn't answered the door."

Stella sighed, locking eyes with Levi. "She's not just working from home, Levi. She's already moved to our overseas branch."

Levi felt his heart plummet. It was as if the air had been sucked out of the room, leaving him gasping for understanding. "Why didn't you tell me this sooner, Stella? You know she means everything to me!"

"Khynzy made me promise not to tell you," Stella said, her voice tinged with a steely resolve. "And, given the circumstances, I don't blame her for wanting to put as much distance between you two as possible. It sounds like you messed up, big time."

Levi's defences crumbled, and he had to steady himself against the meeting room wall. "Do you know where she is staying? I need to follow her. I can't lose her, Stella. I have to make things right."

Stella's expression was strained with exasperation. "Levi, listen to me. As much as you want to chase after her, you need to give her space. If there's any hope of healing this relationship, it must be on her terms, not yours. Following her now would only be an act of selfish desperation."

Levi closed his eyes momentarily, grappling with the immense weight of Stella's words. When he reopened them, they were tinged with the beginnings of acceptance. "You're right, Stella. I've been selfish enough. It's time to think about what's best for Khynzy, even if that means letting her go."

Walking away from the meeting room, each step felt like a mile, each breath like lifting a weight. He was leaving behind more than just a disheartening conversation; he was leaving behind a significant chapter of his life, one filled with love and difficult lessons learned at an almost unbearable cost.

As he returned to his empty desk, Levi understood, perhaps for the first time, that love wasn't solely about holding on. Sometimes, it was about letting go and respecting the chasms and oceans that life puts between you, no matter how agonising the distance.

47

Drowning Regrets

The bar was nestled in the heart of the city, surrounded by the relentless pace of urban life. Inside, a subtle melody blended with muted conversations and the faint scent of old wood mixed with the various liquors on display.

Levi stared into his whiskey, the amber liquid reflecting the neon lights from outside. Memories of Khynzy flooded his mind, from their playful banter to the gentle moments they shared under the stars. Her absence felt like an unending night, one that held no promise of dawn.

Owen, opposite him, took a sip from his beer, his brows furrowed. "You've been staring into that glass for a solid ten minutes," he remarked, attempting to lighten the mood. "Trying to see your future in that whiskey?"

Levi smirked briefly but didn't retort. Owen's jest fell flat, given the weight of what was unsaid between them. Owen cleared his throat, "Alright, man. What's eating you up? I haven't seen you this down since... well, ever."

Drawing a deep breath, Levi murmured, "Khynzy and I... we've broken up."

Owen spat out his beer in disbelief, "What? You two were the definition of relationship goals! What happened?"

Levi hesitated. His secret ability was now more like a curse than a blessing. Having revealed it to Khynzy had torn them apart, and he wasn't prepared to jeopardise his relationship with Owen. He began cautiously, "I need to take you back to when I was nearing thirteen. My family and I were stuck at the airport; our flight was overbooked, and we had to wait hours for the next one. I needed to use the men's room, but all the ones I checked were crowded. After much walking, I finally found this almost hidden one."

He continued, "As I walked in, I saw a man talking on his phone. My headset was on, so he didn't think I could hear him. But in reality, I wasn't playing any music. I just wanted him to think I couldn't hear anything. So I pretended not to listen, but I heard every word. He was talking about hacking into a plane's software."

Owen's brows furrowed in shock. "That's chilling. What did you do?"

With a pained look, Levi admitted, "I was young, naive. I didn't know what to do. An hour after that, a plane exploded mid-air. It was the flight we were supposed to be on."

Owen was silent for a moment, absorbing the heavy weight of Levi's words. His eyes widened with shock and concern as he realised the magnitude of what Levi had just shared. Finally, he found his voice, "Levi, that's... that's unbelievable. I can't even imagine how you must have felt, realising you could have been on that flight."

Owen drew a shaky breath, trying to connect the dots, "That's haunting, but I don't see its relation to Khynzy. Why end things over an old incident?"

Levi avoided Owen's gaze. "That plane? It had Khynzy's parents onboard."

The realisation hit Owen hard. "Oh, Levi... I had no clue."

Sipping his drink, Levi's voice was a mere whisper, "She recently found out. She believes I could've prevented it, maybe reported it to security."

Owen's mind raced, grappling with the enormity. "Levi, you were just a kid! That's too much responsibility for anyone that age."

Levi's eyes shimmered with tears, "There's more to it, things I can't divulge right now."

Owen's protective instincts flared up. "You've always been there for me, and now it's my turn. Regardless of what you can't tell me, know that I've got your back."

The bar's atmosphere thickened with tension. Once playful and inviting, the neon lights now felt harsh and judgmental. Levi whispered, "Thanks, Owen. I wish I could rewind time, set things straight."

Owen stared at the bubbling liquid in his glass, lost in thought.

"I still can't believe it," Owen finally broke the silence, struggling to keep his voice steady. "That plane crash... And to think Khynzy's parents were on that plane."

A weighty silence descended between them, both lost in thoughts of what might have been. Owen took a deep breath, the weight of the revelation heavy on his mind. He cast a sideways glance at Levi, noting his friend's downcast eyes.

Leaving his drink untouched, Owen leaned forward, elbows resting on the scarred wooden table. "What are you planning to do next, Levi? You can't carry this guilt with you forever."

Levi hesitated, picking at the label on his beer bottle. "I don't know, Owen. Right now, everything feels... empty. I thought about maybe following Khynzy to the overseas branch, try to fix things there."

Owen raised an eyebrow. "You really think that's a good idea? Sometimes, space is what two people need to heal. And honestly, after a revelation like that, I think both of you could use a breather."

Levi's gaze fell to his drink. "But I can't just let her go, Owen. There's no one else like her. Everywhere I look, I see memories of her."

Owen tried to hide the concern etching his features. "Look, Levi, I get it. She's special. But if you're considering chasing after her, you better be sure it's for the right reasons. Not just out of guilt or because you feel you have to."

Levi sighed, "I know, I know. It's just..."

Owen interrupted, "If you're thinking about moving on or finding a rebound, I'm here for you, mate. We can hit the clubs, find you someone to take your mind off things."

Levi chuckled weakly, "Rebound? Really? That's your solution?"

"Hey, it's just a suggestion," Owen grinned, trying to lighten the mood. "But seriously, you need to think about what's best for both of you."

Levi nodded, taking a deep breath. "I just miss her, Owen. Every day. But you're right. Maybe we both need some space to figure things out."

Owen clapped Levi on the back. "That's the spirit. Time heals, bro. And who knows? Maybe one day, you two will find your way back to each other."

Levi smiled, a faint glimmer of hope lighting up his eyes. "Thanks, Owen. I needed to hear that."

The two friends spent the rest of the evening reminiscing about better times, finding solace in shared memories and the bond of brotherhood. But as the night deepened, Levi's thoughts inevitably drifted back to Khynzy, wondering what the future held for them both.

48

The Silent Phone

Levi sat at his workstation, surrounded by dual monitors flashing with lines of code. He'd been deep in collaboration with a developer, tirelessly working to debug an intricate issue for the better part of the day. Each line they dissected, every error they encountered, seemed like a puzzle demanding immediate attention. And yet, for all the concentration he tried to muster, his thoughts would invariably wander. They drifted to Khynzy, her laughter, the way her eyes would light up in a discussion, and the countless memories they had shared. The digital maze in front of him blurred for a moment as he lost himself in a sea of reminiscence.

His phone lay on the desk beside his keyboard. It was strategically placed so he could see it even when engrossed in his work. He had set a special notification tone for messages from Khynzy, a tone he hadn't heard in weeks now. Yet he couldn't help but glance at the phone every few minutes, each time a tiny ember of hope ignited and quickly extinguished by the screen's unyielding emptiness.

As he was about to delve back into his work, his phone buzzed. His heart skipped a beat as he snatched it up, but the notification on the screen wasn't what he yearned for. It was just an email from HR about an upcoming team-building event. A wave of disappointment washed over him, and he set the phone back down, its screen going dark along with his brief flicker of hope.

Finally accepting that his concentration was irrevocably fractured, he locked his computer and gathered his belongings. It was time to leave, but the prospect of going home to an empty apartment was equally daunting. Yet, what options did he have?

Walking through the dimly lit parking garage to his car, he felt enveloped by a similar darkness within. Upon entering his car, the empty passenger seat seemed to mock him once more. It was as though the universe was ensuring he could not escape reminders of his solitude, even within the confined spaces he used to share with the woman he still deeply loved.

The phone remained silent, a cruel mirror reflecting the silence that filled his life ever since Khynzy walked away. As he drove off, each passing streetlight seemed to illuminate his isolation, casting fleeting shadows that felt like the ghosts of his past, whispering of a love that had grown silent.

Finally, Levi parked his car and made his way into his apartment. He flung his keys onto the kitchen counter, sank onto the couch, and pulled out his phone. Opening his photo gallery, he scrolled through pictures of happier times: vacations they'd taken, meals they'd shared, and simple moments captured on lazy Sunday mornings. His finger hovered over a photo where they were both laughing, her eyes twinkling with a joy that now seemed worlds away.

For a fleeting moment, he thought about deleting the photos, as if doing so would make the pain of her absence easier to bear. But he couldn't bring himself to press that unforgiving trash icon. The photos were a cruel paradox, both a tether to the happiness he once felt and a glaring reminder of the emptiness that had replaced it.

Levi moved to his home office and sat at his desk, glancing at the empty chair across from him and then at his phone. For a while, he had obsessively checked Khynzy's social media updates, seeking any glimpse into her new life overseas. But those updates had stopped appearing. It's been quite a while since her last livestream of a drum cover too. Whether she had changed her privacy settings or simply stopped posting, he couldn't tell. The absence of her digital presence felt like a second loss, a confirmation of the distance that had grown between them.

His phone remained silent, its screen dark, mirroring the void he felt inside. He placed it face-down, unable to bear the weight of its silence any longer. No calls, no messages, no social media updates—only a vacuum where her voice, her laughter, and her thoughts used to be.

As the night grew darker, the silence became a loud, resonating emptiness, echoing the hollow space that Khynzy had left behind.

49

I Need a Moment

Levi sat in his living room, guitar in hand, softly strumming the chords to a song he used to jam with Khynzy. As he played, memories flooded back—Khynzy behind the drum set, her face flushed with excitement, her white tank top clinging to her skin, and those torn denim shorts that he loved so much. The nostalgia was almost overwhelming.

I need a moment, he thought to himself.

After setting his guitar carefully against the couch, Levi walked over to the window and closed the blinds. Assured of his privacy, he sat back down. His eyes briefly caught the glow of the chandelier above him—a fixture that Khynzy had once fallen in love with, a lingering piece of their past that still adorned his living room.

His thoughts naturally drifted to her—how her tank top emphasised her curves and how her denim shorts showcased her smooth and elegantly proportioned legs. He glanced down at his hands, taking a slow, steadying breath. As he looked back up, his eyes met the chandelier again, its light tinged with memories, almost as if it too had a story to tell. As his head rested against the backrest of the couch, he closed his eyes, taking deep breaths, losing himself in these significant moments.

Eventually, he stood and walked to the bathroom. Washing his hands at the sink, he felt a newfound calmness envelop him. He returned to the couch and picked up the guitar again but couldn't bring himself to continue the song.

❧

A few days later, Levi was scrolling through old files on his computer at his home office when he stumbled upon a folder of photos from years past. One caught his eye—it was a picture of him and Khynzy at the company Christmas ball. She wore a teal evening gown that made her look like a movie star. Levi remembered how every guy in the room seemed to be looking at her that night, and for a brief moment, they all wished they were him. It was the night they had taken their relationship to the next level, right in this apartment.

"I need a moment," he whispered to himself. His finger hesitated over the touchpad before zooming in on her image. His breathing grew heavier.

After some time, he abruptly closed the lid of his laptop, took a deep breath to regain his composure, and walked over to the bathroom sink. He turned on the tap and washed his hands, allowing the water to cleanse away the emotional weight he had just experienced.

❧

A week later, Levi decided it was time to declutter. His hand touched something silky as he rummaged through a box of old clothes in his closet. Pulling it out, he found Khynzy's satin sleep shorts. Holding the fabric, memories of laughter-filled movie nights at home swarmed him. He remembered how those shorts looked on her, usually paired with one of his t-shirts, which were oversized on her frame.

I need a moment, he thought, laying the shorts beside him on the bed.

Levi sat still for a while, letting memories wash over him

like a wave. Eventually, he walked to the bathroom and washed his hands. He came back out, folded the shorts meticulously, and tucked them away in a keepsake box at the back of his closet. He felt a quiet focus take over him as he resumed sorting through the rest of his belongings.

❧

The following Saturday night, Levi was out with friends. As he watched couples around him engage in public displays of affection, his thoughts inevitably drifted to Khynzy. She might not be the life of the party, but her beauty and quiet charm had a magnetic effect. Levi remembered how her presence stood out to him even in a crowded room, making everything else seem less important.

"I need a moment," he told his friends, excusing himself.

Levi made his way to the restroom and closed the door behind him. After some time, he finally turned on the tap and washed his hands thoroughly. When he returned to the table, he felt a little more composed yet still wistful.

❧

One Thursday night, shortly after arriving home from work, Levi was alone on the same old couch, aimlessly watching TV. His thoughts drifted back to their movie marathons, the two of them cuddled up right here. She would laugh at the funny parts and snuggle closer during the sentimental scenes. They often lost interest in the movie, turning their attention to each other.

He loosened his tie and opened the top button of his shirt as if trying to physically relieve the emotional pressure building up inside him. "I need a moment," he sighed.

Turning off the TV, he got up to close the blinds, casting the room into semi-darkness, and went back to the couch. After some time, he walked to the kitchen sink to wash his hands, reopened the blinds, and turned the TV back on.

The sound from the TV filled the room with chatter and laughter that he barely registered. His eyes were drawn to the empty seat beside him on the couch—a space where laughter and love once lived. He realised he would rather have that seat remain empty than be filled by anyone other than Khynzy.

50

The Hollow Title

Most would have expected his work performance to falter, especially with the emotional toll of losing Khynzy. But the opposite happened. In a way, his solitude forged his focus and determination. Levi poured himself into his projects, wielding his technical prowess like never before, as if he could fill the empty spaces in his life with lines of code and architectural designs.

The atmosphere in the conference room buzzed with energy. Teammates, colleagues, and executives all gathered as Levi stood at the front. He had just been promoted to Lead Software Architect—a remarkable achievement that spoke volumes about his professional journey.

"Levi, you've proven yourself to be invaluable," his boss began, handing him a plaque engraved with "Excellence in Leadership." "Your technical mastery and team guidance have been second to none. As Lead Software Architect, we're confident you'll steer this ship to even greater heights."

Amid the applause and congratulatory remarks, Levi felt a complex mixture of pride and emptiness. His words of gratitude to his team seemed to hang in the air as he spoke them, each syllable tinged with a sense of what could have been.

Levi was escorted to his new office, a spacious room adorned with modern furniture and equipped with cutting-edge technology. The door closed behind him, and he found himself alone in this newly designated sanctum. As he settled into his ergonomically designed chair, a void lingered. The room was pristine, modern, and distinctly his, yet its very newness emphasised its lack of her presence.

As the evening wound down, his phone buzzed with congratulatory messages. Friends, family, and colleagues sent their well-wishes, making his promotion social media official. Yet each new notification led to a fleeting hope that her name would appear on the screen—a hope that went unfulfilled.

Later, a company newsletter popped into his inbox. Scrolling down, he saw a section highlighting the achievements of employees in overseas branches. His eyes paused on Khynzy's name, followed by a list of her accomplishments. A swell of pride washed over him, mixed with an ache he couldn't shake off.

Levi took a moment to sit back, feeling the weight of his new title as both a milestone and a millstone. With every step up the career ladder, the absence of the person who had once been his greatest support became increasingly palpable. At that moment, he realised that no amount of professional success could fill the emotional vacancy she had left behind. Even as the Lead Software Architect with his own office, his blueprint for happiness felt woefully incomplete.

His eyes drifted to the cityscape beyond his office window. The skyline was dotted with lights, each one a distant star in an urban universe that felt somehow incomplete. Years had passed, yet the space Khynzy had left seemed to grow rather than shrink with time.

He found himself questioning, as he often did, whether she'd ever come back. What if, by some twist of fate or a change of heart, she decided to return? Would they pick up where they left off or had too much time passed? These questions had become a mental loop, playing in the background of his mind, sometimes taking centre stage when he was least prepared for them.

His phone buzzed again, snapping him back to the present. It was a calendar reminder for a team meeting he had to lead the next day. Professional responsibilities continued to pile up, but none of them could fill the void that had been a part of him for four long years.

Sighing, he locked his computer and prepared to leave the office. As he did, his eyes caught a framed photo on a bookshelf—a candid shot taken at a company event years ago. He and Khynzy were in it, both smiling as if the world was entirely theirs. For a moment, his heart felt impossibly heavy.

Levi turned off the lights and locked his office door behind him. As he walked down the deserted corridor, the weight of his new title and the emptiness of his emotional landscape merged into a singular, haunting question: "Will she ever come back?"

And so, he stepped into the lift, descending not just to the ground floor but also into the depths of his unresolved feelings, realising that no promotion, accolade, or milestone could ever answer that question. With each passing floor, he felt both further from and closer to the answer, suspended in a limbo that years and success had yet to resolve.

51

Dream Home

Beneath the vastness of the azure sky, Levi and Owen strolled toward the latest city jewel: a batch of freshly constructed houses, its modern allure beckoning to prospective buyers. Owen, generally a bubbling fountain of excitement during such ventures, tempered his enthusiasm, attuned to the sombre cloud enveloping Levi. Four years had passed, yet the melancholic haze lingering in Levi's eyes remained as dense as the day Khynzy walked away.

Attempting to penetrate the melancholy, Owen nudged Levi, offering a gentle reminder, "Hey, remember the good old rule, bro? New place, new memories." Levi offered a faint nod; his thoughts ensnared in the haunting 'what ifs' and 'if onlys' that lingered from a past relationship.

Upon stepping into the luminously lit, two-story house, they were immediately swallowed by its modern elegance and an unexpected cascade of memories. Owen, with an investor's keen eye, had invited Levi to join him, contemplating an investment into the newly built house. High ceilings, caressed by recessed lighting, arched above them, casting a warm glow on the sleek furniture and plush, neutral-toned rug in the living area. To Levi, however, the walls, adorned with abstract art, were silent witnesses to not just the space's contemporary allure but to bittersweet memories of a dream home envisioned with Khynzy. His eyes lingered, caught between the past and the potential of a future, prompting Owen to glance back, mildly surprised by his unexpected interest.

As they perused through the house, every room seemed to whisper tales of what could have been. The kitchen was a spectacle of modernity, with its high-gloss white cabinetry, seamlessly integrated appliances, and a strikingly minimalist quartz island. Levi's mind involuntarily painted a picture of Khynzy gleefully dancing around this culinary haven, her laughter echoing amidst the subtle aroma of their collaborative cooking ventures.

The next room they encountered was spacious and soundproof, and to Levi, it spoke volumes. He envisioned Khynzy, her eyes gleaming and energy unbridled, drumming energetically, while his guitars stood proudly in the adjacent corner. The next room, a cosy movie/game room, conjured images of Levi and Khynzy intertwined in a cocoon of love and warmth, surrendering to cinematic tales and shared whispers.

Seeing Levi lost in thought throughout the tour of the house, Owen sensed Khynzy's invisible presence in his friend's musings. In the living room, Levi, donning a sad smile, inquired about the possibility of swapping a light fixture for a chandelier - a nod to Khynzy's love for them.

As they ascended the glass and steel staircase to the second floor, Levi's eyes lingered on the tasteful touches of elegance evident in every nook - from the polished chrome balustrades to the minimalist wall sconces that threw soft shadows on the pristine walls. Each bedroom they encountered unfolded a canvas of chic interior design, with minimalist bed frames, luxurious linens, and panoramic windows that both beckoned and taunted Levi's fractured heart. Two bedrooms whispered promises to Levi, one of a future with Khynzy and the other of a child they had planned to have.

The terrace was the final piece, big enough for parties under the stars, where Levi and Khynzy might have celebrated with their loved ones.

Sensing the emotions in the air, the agent gave them a moment. Owen gently said to Levi, "This is the place you and Khynzy dreamed of, isn't it?"

Levi whispered, voice barely more than a breath, "Yes, Owen. Every corner is filled with our dreams."

Comforting Levi, Owen offered, "You don't have to decide now, Levi. But if it feels right, maybe it's a step towards a future where dreams can still happen."

Choosing to hold on to a fragment of the future they had once dreamt of, Levi decided, "I'll take it, Owen. Maybe some dreams need a place to live, even if they're just memories."

Understanding, Owen supported Levi's choice, quietly pondering if the whispered dreams within the house might someday weave back into reality.

52

Rekindled Hopes

Four years and nine months felt like both a lifetime and a brief interlude as Levi sat at his executive desk, scanning through his emails. His career had taken off, but the ascent had been lonely. Then, an email from a development manager caught his eye—McKhynzy Skylyght is returning to the main branch. His heart pounded in his chest as if trying to break free, a sudden surge of emotions overwhelming him.

He stood up abruptly, pacing around his spacious office. It was as if the universe had decided to hand him both an olive branch and a ticking time bomb. For days, he was restless. Work presentations and meetings blurred into one another, but his thoughts always returned to Khynzy. He wondered how she'd been and if she ever thought of him. More than anything, he wondered if she'd forgiven him.

When his phone vibrated with a call from Owen, his attention snapped to the bright screen. His reaction was neutral and comfortable; it was Owen, his best friend. Answering the call, he greeted, "Hey, Owen."

"Levi, you'll never guess who's back in town," Owen declared, a teasing lilt in his voice.

A peculiar mix of hope and unease brushed against Levi's

heart. Tentatively, he asked, "Who?"

"Khynzy." Owen divulged, pausing to let the information sink in.

Levi nodded slightly. "I heard. A development manager emailed about her transferring back to our main branch."

"But did you know," Owen continued, "she's looking for a place to stay? She wants to rent before deciding to buy."

Levi's thoughts raced. Without pausing, he blurted, "She can rent my new place."

Owen hesitated. "Levi, are you sure about this?"

Levi's voice was firm, yet there was an undercurrent of vulnerability. "Yes, but she can't know I'm the owner. And Owen, offer it at a generous rate. Low, but not so low it raises eyebrows."

Understanding the delicate history, Owen agreed. "Alright. I'll have Ava, one of my agents, handle everything subtly. Khynzy won't suspect a thing, and the rent will just seem like a good deal."

❦

Days later, Khynzy, unknowing of the invisible strings being pulled behind the scenes, stood in the centre of the elegant yet cosy two-story house. Her eyes were drawn upward to a sleek chandelier in the living room, its design a harmonious blend of simplicity and elegance, typical of modern decor. The light fixture's understated sophistication captured the ambience she cherished. Ava, her agent, observed the quiet elation on Khynzy's face. In a murmur that filled the airy space, Khynzy affirmed, "It's perfect," her affirmation as much about the home as the symbolic centrepiece above her.

❦

Finally, the day of Khynzy's return to the main office branch arrived. Levi came in an hour earlier than usual. He wore his best suit, a tailored piece he usually reserved for critical business meetings. On his wrist, he sported the deep blue watch with a gleaming silver bezel – one of the couple watches they had gifted each other for their shared birthday. As he straightened his tie one last time in the mirror, he paused to look at himself. His reflection seemed to question him: Was he ready for this?

When Khynzy entered the office, the world seemed to stand still. She was the same yet different, her eyes holding stories that he was not a part of. He stepped forward, his heart in his throat.

"Welcome back, Khynzy," he managed to say, extending a hand.

"Thank you, Levi," she replied, shaking his hand with a firm grip. As their hands met, a cascade of memories flooded back, a mix of nostalgia and lingering pain swirling in their grasp. His palm was warm and firm, a reminder of a closeness once shared. Her touch sent a jolt through him, a spark of the love that still smouldered in the recesses of his heart. It was a handshake laden with unsaid words, a silent dance of fingers whispering of lost chances and hopeful yearnings.

"It's good to be back." Their eyes locked for a fleeting moment, a silent conversation exchanged, before they reluctantly withdrew their hands, the air around them tinged with a melancholy sweetness.

Khynzy moved on to greet the other team members, her laughter echoing around the room as she reacquainted herself with old friends and met new colleagues. The sight of her smiling and talking to others was a bittersweet sight for Levi. For years, he had imagined scenarios where they'd meet again, and now that it was happening, the reality was far more complicated than any fantasy.

During the staff meeting later that day, Levi found himself inadvertently glancing at Khynzy. Their eyes met once, a spark of shared history flashing between them before they both looked away. Business discussions flowed around them, but the real conversation, the one that mattered most, remained unspoken.

After the meeting dispersed, Levi returned to his office, sinking into his chair with a sigh. On his desk were stacks of reports and an endless list of emails demanding his attention, but all he could focus on was the woman in the adjacent room who had once been his everything.

He had never stopped loving her. That much was clear. Now, the ball was in both their courts. Could they move past their history, and did they even want to?

As the workday drew close, Levi felt more uncertain than he had in years. Yet, beneath the layers of doubt and apprehension, lay a sliver of hope. And that hope was powerful enough to make him believe that the future, while uncertain, held a promise worth exploring.

So, with a renewed sense of purpose, Levi prepared to navigate the complicated terrain ahead. It wouldn't be easy, but for the first time in years, he felt ready to face whatever challenges and opportunities lay on the horizon.

53

Take Your Kids to Work Day

The office was transformed. Colourful balloons floated near the ceiling, the cheerful screams and laughter of children resonated through the hallways, and tables filled with art supplies and snacks were spread across communal areas. It was 'Take Your Kids to Work Day', a much-awaited event during the school holidays where employees could bring their children to work.

Levi felt a pang of loneliness as he watched his colleagues interact with their families. Kids drew pictures, played games, and devoured cookies, all while their parents snapped photos and made small talk. Despite the buzz of activity, Levi's spacious office felt like an island of solitude in a sea of familial joy.

He had been going through emails when a colleague knocked on his open door. "Hey, did you see that Khynzy brought her son today?" The question was innocent, but it struck Levi like a bolt of lightning.

"Her son?" The words stuck in his throat, heavy with an emotion he couldn't quite identify. A jumble of feelings—pain, envy, and an acute sense of loss—overwhelmed him. He had spent almost five years missing Khynzy, incapable of forming a meaningful relationship with anyone else because they all paled in comparison to what he had once had with her. And now she had a son, a family, without him.

Needing to see for himself, Levi rose from his chair and walked across the office. He stopped at a distance, far enough not to be noticed but close enough to observe. There was Khynzy, radiant as ever, chatting with Stella. Next to her was a young boy, deeply engrossed in his colouring book. A whirlpool of emotions sucked him deeper into his thoughts. The child was a vivid reminder of the family Khynzy had built—a family that he wasn't a part of.

The boy looked up, and for a moment, their blue eyes met. The youngster's gaze was innocently curious, but to Levi, it felt like an X-ray probing his soul. What did this child mean in Khynzy's life? And where did that leave him?

Realising he'd been staring, Levi quickly looked away as Khynzy's gaze shifted towards him. For a second, their eyes met, each knowing that the other had recognised the silent exchange. The atmosphere felt thick, laden with unspoken words and unresolved emotions.

Returning to his office, Levi closed the door and closed his eyes. He felt like an observer of a life that could've, should've, been his. And the realisation was gut-wrenching. There, in his spacious office, surrounded by accolades and reminders of his professional success, he'd never felt more incomplete.

He found his chair and sank into it, his mind awash with contemplation. The sharp contrast between his solitude and the communal joy outside his door left him questioning the choices that had brought him to this point. In a life so seemingly filled with achievement, why did he feel like he had lost so much?

He began to consider what his life had become—a series of accomplishments that felt increasingly hollow. He hadn't allowed himself the opportunity to move on, let alone the courage to forgive himself. And now, Khynzy had returned with a visual representation of a future she'd built without him.

54

The Resonance of Silence

Levi sat alone in his office, wrestling with a swirl of complex emotions. He glanced down at the watch on his wrist, and after a moment's hesitation, he carefully took it off and placed it atop his desk. He hardly noticed his door slightly ajar until a small, curious face peered through the gap. A little boy cautiously stepped in. With him came an absence of thought noise, a silence Levi had only ever experienced with Khynzy.

"Hi," the boy greeted, holding a toy dinosaur tightly. "Your office looks cool!"

Levi approached the boy, bending down to meet the child's eyes. Levi felt a smile break through his emotional fog. "Thank you. What's your name?"

"Blue," the boy announced proudly.

As he looked at Blue, Levi couldn't help but notice their similarities. The shape and colour of his eyes, the curve of his smile; could it be? A flicker of hope sparked in his chest, changing the colour of his mood. "Nice to meet you, Blue. I see you've got a dinosaur there. What kind is it?"

"It's a T-Rex!" Blue replied, holding the toy up for Levi to see. "He's the king of dinosaurs."

"Ah, the T-Rex is a fine choice," Levi said, his excitement

building. "What do you want to be when you grow up? A dinosaur detective?"

"No, I want to be an astronaut!" Blue exclaimed, his blue eyes shining with excitement. "I want to see the stars up close!"

"That's a fantastic dream," Levi said, standing up. "You know, it's never too early to shoot for the stars."

"Are you hungry?" Levi asked, feeling more animated than he had in days. "I have a stash of snacks here."

Blue's eyes widened. "Really? What do you have?"

Levi opened the cabinet to reveal an assortment of snacks —granola bars, packets of nuts, and fruit snacks. "How about a granola bar? It's a chocolate chip."

Blue grinned. "Yes, please!"

Handing over the snack, Levi watched as Blue eagerly tore into the wrapper.

"Do you know who I am?" Levi then asked, unable to contain his anticipation. "My name is Levi."

Blue's face lit up like the morning sun. Rushing forward, the little boy wrapped his arms around Levi's legs and exclaimed, "I know! Papa!"

The word electrified Levi's world. He bent down and hugged Blue tightly, his heart swelling with hope and joy. "Papa? Why would you say that?"

Blue shrugged as he pulled away and picked up his toy. "Mama thinks it. I heard her."

The words intrigued Levi. Could Blue also hear thoughts like he could? He stored that question away for later, filing it next to his surging hope.

Before Levi could delve further into the emotional whirlpool that Blue's statement had stirred, a soft knock sounded at the door. Khynzy stood on the threshold, her eyes widening in surprise as they met Levi's.

"I hope he hasn't been a bother," she said, her voice tinged with apprehension and curiosity.

Levi shook his head, a newfound brightness in his eyes. "No, not at all. Blue and I were just talking about dinosaurs, dreams, and snacks."

"We should catch up," Khynzy said, her eyes lingering on Levi's transformed expression. "Absolutely," Levi agreed, rising to his full height. "I've missed our conversations."

Khynzy's eyes met Levi's, and in that brief moment, both felt the resonance of years gone by and those yet to come. She glanced down at Blue, who was clutching his T-Rex and granola bar, his eyes darting between his mother and Levi. "By the way," she said, turning back to Levi, "I wanted to invite you to Blue's 4th birthday party this Saturday. We're celebrating it a day after his actual birthday."

The invitation felt like the start of something yet to be created. Levi looked down at Blue and then back at Khynzy. "I'd be honoured to come. It sounds like a special day."

"It will be," Khynzy responded softly. "And it would mean a lot to both of us if you could be there."

Feeling the weight behind her words, Levi nodded. "I wouldn't miss it for the world."

As Khynzy took a step back to leave, Blue scampered towards her, T-Rex in one hand and remnants of his granola bar in the other. "Say bye, Blue," she prompted.

"Bye, Papa!" Blue chirped, his voice filled with affection. *Why is Blue calling Levi 'Papa' when I haven't told him who his father is yet?* The question lingered in Khynzy's mind, though she didn't voice it. Then, with a hopeful glint in Blue's eyes, he added, "Papa, can you come to my real birthday on Friday too?"

Khynzy's heart skipped a beat, caught off guard. She looked at Levi, her eyes searching for a reaction.

Levi, however, was focused on Blue. "I'd love to, buddy," he said, his voice steady.

"But that's a work day," Khynzy interjected, a hint of concern in her voice.

Levi turned to her, his expression thoughtful. "Are you working that day?"

Khynzy shook her head. "No, I'm taking the day off to spend it with Blue."

Levi nodded, making up his mind. "I haven't taken a day off in years. It'll probably be alright for me to take Friday off too."

Levi looked at Blue. The added invitation, innocent as it was, felt like another pivotal moment. "I promise, buddy, I'll be there both days," he said, a feeling of completeness washing over him that he hadn't felt in years.

As Khynzy led Blue out, Levi was left alone in his office, his heart pounding in a rhythm of conflicted emotions. The door closed softly behind them, but the resonance of that moment lingered in the room like a gentle echo.

55

The Calculus of Fatherhood

After Khynzy and Blue had left, Levi's eyes landed on the watch atop his desk. He picked it up, feeling its familiar weight and cool metal. Carefully, he put it back on his wrist. As he fastened it, memories surged. The breakup with Khynzy had been just shy of five years ago. Counting back, it was almost four years and nine months. They had been intimate mere days before everything unravelled between them.

His heart quickened as the pieces fell into place; he felt like he was tiptoeing along the edge of a revelation, balancing between hope and the fear of disappointment. Could he really be Blue's father? The boy's resemblance to him, that unmistakable sense of connection, and now the timing—it was as if the universe was shouting at him, unable to make itself any clearer.

Levi was overcome with a rush of conflicting emotions. The idea that he could have a son, a living piece of himself and Khynzy combined, filled him with a sense of completeness he'd been missing for years. At the same time, the weight of missed moments and lost years pressed upon him. Why didn't Khynzy tell him? Who took care of her when she was pregnant? How would Khynzy react to him wanting to be a real part of their lives?

Levi felt a newfound sense of resolve as he wrestled with these thoughts. He wanted to be Blue's father, not just in name but in every way that mattered. He knew the journey would be fraught with complexities, but the destination seemed worth every obstacle.

His decision made; Levi closed his laptop and switched off the lights in his office. For the first time in years, he left work feeling not like a man burdened with unanswered questions but like one who had found a missing piece of a puzzle he didn't even know he was completing.

As he walked out, the resonance of silence was replaced by a joyful symphony that only he could hear, filled with the promises and perils of a future that he was now eager to embrace. For Levi, the calculus of fatherhood had just begun, and he couldn't wait to see where this new equation would lead.

Levi couldn't help but chuckle at the name "Blue Skylyght," thinking about Khynzy's knack for the whimsical. But as whimsical as it sounded, he couldn't help but think it would sound even better as "Blue Moonstrider." The thought of his potential son carrying his last name felt both hilarious and deeply sentimental. It was like a strange daydream where the universe decided to be a bit more poetic than usual.

"Astronaut Blue Moonstrider reporting for duty," he whispered to himself, grinning as he envisioned a little boy in a spacesuit, ready to conquer uncharted territories—just like he hoped to conquer the uncharted territory of fatherhood.

Shaking his head as if to clear it of these daydreams, he got into his car and drove straight to a nearby toy store. His heart was light, and the burden that had rested on his shoulders for years seemed lifted, if only temporarily.

Walking through the aisles, he gravitated towards the

section filled with dinosaur action figures and space-themed toys. His eyes gleamed at the sight of a T-Rex model that roared when you pressed a button and astronaut gear, complete with a miniature helmet and boots. "Blue would love these," he thought, clutching the toys as if they were sacred artefacts.

He bought far more than any four-year-old could possibly need, but he couldn't care less. Every toy felt like a step closer to a future where he could teach his son about the Jurassic era or the moon landing. It was as if he was trying to cram years of missed opportunities into a single shopping cart, hoping these material items could pave the way to a deeper emotional connection.

When he reached the counter, the cashier eyed the mountain of toys and shot him a curious look. "Someone's going to have an amazing birthday."

Levi smiled, his eyes twinkling with a secret only he was privy to. "You have no idea," he replied, casually waving his card over the reader, the transaction completing with a soft beep.

As he loaded the toys into his car, Levi thought about how strange and wondrous life could be. It was full of unexpected turns, like mysterious algorithms that led to unforeseen outcomes. But for the first time in a long while, Levi felt he was on the brink of solving a problem he hadn't even known existed.

Now, armed with dinosaur toys and astronaut gear, he felt ready to face the challenges and joys that lay ahead. It didn't matter how complicated the equations of life could be; Levi felt like he was finally grasping the right formula. And the first variable in this new equation was, hopefully, a boy named Blue.

56

The Space Between Us

Levi parked his car a few houses away from Khynzy's house, taking a deep breath to calm his jittery nerves. The trunk was packed with the toys he'd bought, each one a silent promise of the life he hoped to share with Blue. He glanced at himself in the rearview mirror, as if seeking approval from the man staring back at him.

In the pocket of his jacket, his phone buzzed — a text from Owen. "She has no clue it's your place, does she?" it read. Before Levi could respond, another message from Owen popped up: "Don't forget to ask Khynzy if I can come to Blue's birthday party." Levi's thumb hovered over the keyboard but opted not to respond, instead tucking the device back into his pocket.

"Here goes nothing," he muttered, stepping out of the car.

He carried the bags of toys, feeling their weight not as a burden but as a testament to his newfound purpose. With each step toward Khynzy's front door, his heart pounded in anticipation, like a drumroll leading up to a life-changing crescendo.

Before he could even knock, the door swung open. Blue's eyes widened, and a squeal of pure delight filled the air.

"Papa!" he exclaimed, running full tilt toward Levi, who had just enough time to set down the bags before scooping the boy into his arms.

For a moment, the world melted away. Levi's arms tightened around Blue, and all the complexities, the what-ifs, and the tangled emotions seemed insignificant. In this precious instant, it was as though the universe had aligned just for them.

Khynzy stood in the doorway, her eyes wide with a mixture of surprise and something unreadable. "Blue, sweetheart, let's give our guest some space, okay?"

"But Mama, it's Papa!" Blue said, wriggling down from Levi's arms but holding onto his hand tightly, worried as if he might vanish into thin air.

Levi met Khynzy's gaze, searching for a clue, any sign that she too felt the gravitational pull that seemed to be drawing him and Blue closer. He saw a glimmer of emotion flash across her eyes before she veiled it with a courteous smile.

"Come in, Levi," she said, stepping aside to let him enter. "Seems like you've brought the entire toy store with you."

He chuckled a bit self-consciously. "Well, let's just say I got carried away."

As they walked into the living room, Blue impatiently tugged at one of the bags, revealing a shiny astronaut helmet. His eyes shone with wonder and excitement, mirroring the stars that adorned the toy.

"This is for me?" he asked, his voice tinged with awe.

"Yes, buddy, all for you," Levi said, kneeling to be at eye level with the boy.

While Blue enthusiastically began exploring his new treasures, Levi turned to Khynzy. The air between them was thick with unspoken words and lingering questions.

"About what Blue has been calling me," he began cautiously, "I've been thinking—"

Khynzy cut him off, her eyes finally meeting his. "We need to talk, don't we?"

He nodded. "Yes, we do."

As they sat on the sofa, Levi's eyes shifted between Khynzy and Blue. The boy was already lost in a world of make-believe, navigating through galaxies and prehistoric jungles with equal zest. And in that moment, Levi realised the stakes of the conversation he was about to have.

Whatever the outcome, whatever the equations or complexities life had in store, one thing was crystal clear: Levi was willing to do whatever it took to be a meaningful part of this picture. Because, cliché or not, it was starting to feel like the family he never knew he needed.

And so, with a deep breath, he turned to Khynzy, ready to open a new chapter in their tangled history. A chapter in which, he hoped, Blue would call him "Papa" not just in innocent child's play but in the meaningful reality they could build together.

But Levi and Khynzy just sat in awkward silence; the tension in the room was palpable. Finally, Blue seemed to notice the silence. He looked up, his eyes moving from Levi to Khynzy and back to Levi. Then, as if coming to a decision, he grabbed the T-Rex model and the astronaut helmet, rushing over to where Levi sat.

"Papa, look! Rawr!" Blue made the T-Rex toy come to life, mimicking a roar that was more adorable than fearsome. "And this one can go to the moon!" He waved the astronaut helmet enthusiastically.

Levi's eyes twinkled as he watched the boy. "That T-Rex doesn't stand a chance against Astronaut Blue," he said, playing along.

Blue giggled, delighted. "You really think so?"

"I know so," Levi affirmed.

Suddenly, Blue dropped the toys, threw his arms around

Levi's neck, and hugged him tightly. "Thank you, Papa! Bestest toys ever!"

Before Levi knew it, Blue had planted a small but heartfelt kiss on his cheek. It was a simple gesture, but the impact was monumental. If emotions had a physical weight, Levi felt like he had just been gifted a treasure chest full of gold.

Khynzy watched the exchange, her eyes misty but smiling. It was as though she could see the invisible threads of connection weaving themselves tighter around her son and Levi.

"Papa, will you play with me? Please?" Blue's eyes were wide, filled with innocent hope.

Levi felt a lump forming in his throat, overwhelmed by the pure love emanating from this tiny being who might be his son. "Of course, buddy. Let's show that T-Rex what Astronaut Blue and his co-pilot are made of."

As they moved to the floor, engrossed in a world where dinosaurs and astronauts coexisted, Levi couldn't help but think that this was the most real thing he'd ever felt. It was as if he had discovered a new form of gravity—a force that pulled him toward Blue, anchoring him to the present moment and to a future full of untapped potential.

As he held a plastic dinosaur in one hand and a toy spaceship in the other, playing with joy and earnestness he hadn't felt in years, Levi knew that he had stumbled upon something extraordinary.

He looked up to find Khynzy watching them, her eyes meeting his. There were still countless words left unsaid, bridges to be crossed, and challenges to face. But for now, in this moment, none of that seemed to matter.

Blue's laughter filled the room, echoing in Levi's heart and soul, banishing the shadows of what-ifs and could-have-beens. And as they played, lost in their shared world, Levi felt the unspoken promise that bound them all together—the promise of a love that, like gravity, required no words, only presence.

57

The Equation of Blue

The smell of garlic and basil wafted through the air as Khynzy took a pan off the stove, placing it on the dining table that was already adorned with bowls of salad, fresh bread, and a hearty pasta dish.

Levi inhaled deeply, letting the familiar aroma fill his senses. He had forgotten how much he missed Khynzy's cooking. "It smells amazing, Zee," he said, realising only after he'd said it how intimate the nickname sounded.

"Thank you," she replied, her eyes meeting his for a fleeting moment before she busied herself with serving the food.

As they sat down to eat, Blue's enthusiasm seemed to bridge the emotional distance between the two adults. With every delightful gasp over a meatball or a sip of apple juice, the atmosphere grew warmer and more relaxed.

Finally, after his third helping of pasta, Blue seemed to hit a wall of exhaustion. His eyes drooped, and his hyperactivity gave way to yawns.

Levi stood up, wiping his mouth with a napkin. "I'll get him ready for bed, if that's okay?"

Khynzy nodded, grateful. "That would be wonderful,

thank you."

Blue, already half-asleep, allowed himself to be scooped up in Levi's arms. They proceeded to the bathroom, where Levi gently bathed him, dressed him in pyjamas, and read him a bedtime story. Blue's room was filled with more dinosaur and space-themed decor, making Levi feel like he had somehow already been a part of this space without even knowing it.

As he tucked Blue in, the little boy mumbled, "Night, Papa," before drifting off to sleep, sealing the end of a surreal but heartfelt day. Levi's eyes lingered on the peaceful face of the child, a sense of tranquillity washing over him.

Returning to the living room, Levi found Khynzy sitting on the sofa, an unreadable expression on her face. This was it—the conversation both had been avoiding yet knew was inevitable.

"Zee, we do need to talk," Levi broke the silence.

Khynzy took a deep breath. "Levi, I'm sorry for not telling you about Blue. I had my reasons, but I know I should have told you."

He waited, not wanting to rush her.

"After my parents' accident, after finding out you could have done something to prevent it, but you didn't try harder, I couldn't bear to be around you. The grief was too raw, too painful. I needed space to heal, to understand," she finally said, her voice tinged with an emotion he couldn't quite place.

Levi nodded, absorbing her words. "I've carried that guilt every day, Zee, and I can never make it right. But Blue—our son—deserves to have both of us in his life."

Khynzy looked up, her eyes meeting his. "I agree. But let's take it slow. Co-parenting to start with. We both need to relearn how to be in each other's lives, especially for Blue's sake."

Levi felt a mix of relief and hope. "I can live with that, as long as it means being a part of Blue's life—and hopefully, in time, a part of yours again too."

Khynzy nodded, the hint of a tear in her eye. "It's a start, Levi. A fragile, complicated start."

"But a start nonetheless," he said softly, thinking of the laughter and love he had shared with Blue earlier and the complex tapestry of emotions he would have to navigate with Khynzy.

Taking a deep breath, Levi ventured, "Zee, do you think Blue is like me or like you? Can he hear what I hear? Does he see auras?"

Khynzy looked startled, then contemplative. "He's still young, Levi. If he has any abilities, they haven't shown yet. Or maybe he doesn't understand what it means."

Levi paused, then added, "When I asked him why he called me 'Papa,' he said, 'Mama thinks it, I heard it.' That got me wondering..."

Khynzy's eyes widened. "If that's the case, then we'll face it, but separately for now. He'll have us both guiding him from our own corners. He won't have to navigate it alone."

Levi caught her gaze, seeing both the possibilities and the barriers between them. For now, they were co-parents, united by their son but divided by the past.

"Whatever comes, we'll figure it out. For Blue's sake."

She nodded, eyes tinged with unshed tears. "Yes. And his full name is Blue Skylyght."

"Skylyght? That's your surname. What about mine?"

Khynzy hesitated for a moment. "When I had to raise him alone, I felt it was best for him to carry my name. But now that you know, it's your choice too."

Levi sighed deeply. "He's got my eyes," he mumbled, recalling the face of the boy he had just tucked into bed.

"Yes, he does," Khynzy said softly, her eyes misting.

Levi looked back at her, his gaze intense. "I want him to

carry the Moonstrider name."

Khynzy nodded, understanding the weight of Levi's words. "Alright, Levi. We'll talk to him about becoming Blue Moonstrider."

As Levi heard her say it out loud, he felt a newfound sense of responsibility and connection. When Khynzy agreed, Levi felt a rush of hope fill him, though he kept it to himself. This was more than just a name change; in his heart, he dared to hope it was a step toward a future where he, Khynzy, and their son could be a family.

As they sat there, not quite a family but no longer mere strangers, Levi felt a cautious optimism take root. The path ahead was complicated, a tangled equation of past mistakes and future promises. But as he looked back on the evening, watching his son sleep and sitting across from the woman he had once loved so deeply, Levi felt like he was finally on the verge of solving it.

After all, every complex equation starts with a single, hopeful variable. And theirs was named Blue.

58

A Birthday Party to Remember

The day following Blue's intimate birthday celebration was a whirlwind of activity. Khynzy's home had been transformed overnight into a bustling hub of party preparations. The terrace, half-covered by a beautifully crafted pergola, became the centrepiece of the festivities. Entwined around the pergola's lattice were twinkling fairy lights, adding a magical glow to the space. From this illuminated framework, stars and various space-related decorations were hung, creating a mesmerizing cosmic canopy. Below this stellar and softly lit display, the terrace floor was adorned with scattered dinosaur figures, seamlessly blending into the "Space-Age Jurassic" theme Blue was so fond of. The combination of fairy lights and thematic decorations under the pergola made for an enchanting and whimsical party setting.

Levi arrived early to help with last-minute arrangements, a sense of excitement pulsing through him. This would be his first time attending one of Blue's birthdays, and the significance wasn't lost on him.

Guests started pouring in—neighbours, friends from Blue's preschool, and some of Khynzy's friends and colleagues. As Blue moved about in a little astronaut costume, complete with a plastic helmet under his arm, the party kicked into full gear.

Levi felt a range of emotions watching Blue socialise, open presents, and even lead the crowd in a dinosaur stomp dance. His eyes frequently met Khynzy's, each glance a silent acknowledgement of the happiness and complexities that swirled around them.

The pinnacle of the party came when a cake shaped like a rocket ship was brought out, complete with smoke effects created by dry ice. As Blue blew out the candles to the tune of "Happy Birthday," the room filled with applause and cheers.

Levi watched his son with a mixture of pride and tender care. His heart was set on making the day unforgettable for Blue.

Among the guests was Owen, Levi's closest friend, his eyes occasionally shifting to a large, covered object in the yard — a special gift for Blue. Approaching Levi, Owen asked quietly, "Have you told your parents about Blue yet?"

Levi paused, considering his words. "Not yet," he replied. "They're on a months-long cruise. I'm sure they'd rush back if they knew, and I don't want to disrupt their trip. I'll tell them once they return. They live in another city, after all."

As Levi finished speaking, Blue rushed towards them, exclaiming, "Papa, I am having so much fun!" Levi's face lit up with a warm smile as he bent down to embrace his son, the joy of the moment enveloping them both. "I'm glad, buddy," he said. Standing up, he turned to Owen. "Blue, I want you to meet someone special. This is Uncle Owen, a very close friend of mine."

Owen, kneeling at Blue's level, couldn't help but observe the striking resemblance between Blue and Levi. *He looks just like Levi,* Owen thought, *but there's a gentleness in his face, maybe from his mom, Khynzy.* He smiled warmly at Blue. "Happy Birthday, little astronaut! I'm Uncle Owen. I brought you something amazing."

Owen led Blue and Levi to the covered object in the yard and with a dramatic flourish,   unveiled the electric space rover—a stunning open-top vehicle, complete with the Space Federation logo and glowing blue lights on its rims. The rover, designed for a child but with impressive attention to detail, was equipped with a seatbelt and a rubber bumper for safety, ensuring it was perfectly suited for young adventurers like Blue. The rover was capped at a safe speed of 8 kilometres per hour, ideal for a child's play.

"Wow! Is that for me?" Blue gasped, his eyes wide with wonder.

"Yes, it's all yours," Owen replied, his voice filled with warmth. "It's a special rover for a special boy. You can drive it around at a safe speed, and don't forget to buckle up!"

Blue eagerly climbed into the driver's seat, fastening the seatbelt with a small click.

Owen patiently showed Blue how to operate the rover. It was designed for ease, with simple buttons for power and sound, and a joystick for navigation. As Blue pressed the button to start, the rover lit up and made engaging sounds, simulating a real space adventure.

With a gentle push on the accelerator, Blue began to drive, his initial cautious movements soon turning into confident steering. Levi watched his son with a mixture of pride and astonishment.

"That looks expensive," Levi observed, admiring the intricate details of the rover as Blue joyously navigated the makeshift moonscape.

Owen chuckled softly, "It's like four birthdays' worth of gifts. I had some catching up to do and I wanted to make it special for Blue."

Watching Blue with a contented smile, Owen felt a familial warmth in his heart. "And seeing him light up like this, that's the real gift," he added. To Owen, Levi was more than just a friend; he was the brother he never had, making Blue akin to a nephew. The joy in Blue's eyes and his laughter were priceless to Owen, far outweighing the monetary value of the rover. The moment underscored the deep bond he shared with Levi, a connection that went beyond mere friendship to something much more profound and enduring.

After a few minutes of joyful exploration, Blue steered the rover back to where Levi and Owen stood. He stopped it gently, turned off the engine, and unbuckled his seatbelt with a practised flick. Then, with a burst of excitement, he jumped out and ran towards Owen, arms outstretched for a hug.

"Thank you, Uncle Owen!" Blue exclaimed, his embrace full of gratitude. Levi watched the scene, his heart swelling with pride and appreciation for Owen's thoughtful and generous gift.

❦

As the party began to wind down and guests said their goodbyes, Levi found himself in the living room, picking up stray wrapping paper and deflated balloons. Khynzy joined him, a tired but content smile on her face.

"We did it," she said, looking around the room as if to take stock of the event and, perhaps, the journey that had led them there.

"We did," Levi agreed. "And it was great."

Blue ran up to them, now rid of his astronaut attire but still buzzing with residual energy. "Papa, Mama, best birthday ever!"

Khynzy bent down to hug Blue. "All thanks to Papa's help, right?"

"Yeah, Papa made it extra special!"

Levi felt a surge of emotion at these simple words. He picked Blue up and swung him into the air, eliciting a joyful squeal from the little boy.

As the evening settled in, and Blue finally succumbed to

his exhaustion—falling asleep on the couch surrounded by his new toys—Levi and Khynzy found themselves alone in the kitchen, cleaning up and storing away leftovers.

"Blue had a fantastic day, and it means a lot that you were here," Khynzy said, her voice tinged with warmth but also a trace of tiredness.

"I wouldn't have missed it for the world," Levi responded, choosing his words carefully. "I hope this is just the beginning, though. I want to be more involved in his life and, if possible, in yours."

Khynzy paused, setting down a stack of plates. "Levi, we have a complicated history, and it's not something we can easily ignore."

"I'm not suggesting we erase the past," Levi interjected, his voice filled with sincerity. "I just want a chance to be a constant presence in both your lives, especially for Blue."

Khynzy met his eyes, her expression softening. "Let's start with co-parenting, for Blue's sake. As for us, I'm not closed off on the idea, but I need a little more time to sort through things. Let's take it step by step."

Her words offered Levi a glimmer of hope, suggesting that the door wasn't entirely closed—just slightly ajar, waiting for the right moment to swing open.

Levi's voice, tender and cautiously optimistic, broke through the gentle hum of the apartment. "Zee, there's something I've held back about this house that you should know."

Her movements stilled, and she met his gaze, a soft questioning in her eyes. "Hmm, what do you mean? What is it?"

He took a steadying breath, his words a gentle revelation. "I bought this house around half a year ago. It reminded me of the dream house we often pictured together. And when I heard from Owen that you were looking for a place to rent, I asked him to suggest my house to you. At that time, I didn't know about Blue."

A quiet, palpable pause lingered as she absorbed the weight of his words, her eyes reflecting a storm of unspoken thoughts and emotions.

"I know you have the means to secure any home you want for yourself and Blue. But now that I know I'm his father, it's very important to me to provide and ensure that you both have a stable home here. So, I hope you'll consider this your permanent home, and of course, you won't need to pay rent."

"Levi, I need time to process this." She whispered, her voice threading through the quietude.

He nodded gently, affirming her need. "Take all the time you need, Zee. And don't worry, I want to assure you..."

Her eyes, cautiously expectant, met his once again.

He spoke, a heartfelt assurance framing his words. "I'm not going to impose myself moving in, unless that's something you want in the future. My priority is the well-being and stability of you and Blue. I'll be here, regardless, in whatever capacity you need me to be."

The lingering silence enveloped them, delicate and filled with the echoes of past dreams and the fragile possibility of future understandings, as they navigated through the complex tapestry of old wounds and tentative reconnections.

As they resumed their cleanup, both were acutely aware of the intricacies that lay ahead. Blue, who had curled up asleep on a cushion, seemed to epitomise the possibilities and complications of this new family dynamic—a vivid reminder of the complex emotional terrain they would have to traverse together, one step at a time.

59

The Weight of Redemption

Despite the emotional distance between Levi and Khynzy after months of co-parenting, today was about their son Blue and perhaps about finding a way back to each other.

"Look, Papa! A dragon!" Blue's youthful exuberance broke through Levi's introspective moment. He pointed to a vividly painted dragon on the carousel, its scales shimmering in the sunlight.

"All right, buddy, let's go tame that dragon," Levi said, lifting Blue onto the fantastical creature.

Across the carousel, Khynzy was capturing the moment on her phone. Her smile was radiant, and for a brief minute, Levi felt transported back to a simpler time. The carousel spun, a merry tune playing, and laughter filled the air.

Next on the agenda was the Ferris wheel. Each carriage had two seats at opposite ends, allowing passengers to face each other. Khynzy was the first to step into the Ferris wheel carriage, followed by Blue, who quickly chose the seat opposite her. Levi, intending to sit next to Blue, was stopped by his son's assertive voice. "Papa, sit with Mama; I'm a big boy now." His words, veiled in childlike innocence, carried a hopeful hint, a silent wish for his parents to be closer, as Levi acquiesced and took the seat next to Khynzy, leaving Blue proudly alone on the opposite one.

As the wheel began its gradual ascent, Levi felt an irresistible pull towards Khynzy, a longing that transcended mere physical attraction. Summoning his courage, he subtly brushed his fingers against hers. The instant their skin touched, a comforting warmth washed over him, reaching even the coldest, most forgotten corners of his heart.

Khynzy felt it too. The simple touch sent a subtle but undeniable current through her, momentarily eclipsing the years of hurt and complexity. It was as if, for that fleeting instant, they could both imagine a world where things were simpler, where their love was all that mattered.

Taking her lack of resistance as a sign, Levi fully grasped her hand. Their fingers intertwined naturally, each one filling the spaces of the other as if designed to fit. It felt like coming home after a long, tumultuous journey.

Their eyes met, and in that brief moment suspended high in the sky, the world beyond them faded, complexities and uncertainties dissolved, leaving only the raw, unspoken connection they both knew still existed between them.

"We're like astronauts up here, Papa," Blue said, his eyes wide with wonder, oblivious to the silent exchange between his parents.

"Absolutely, buddy," Levi replied, still holding Khynzy's hand.

After their Ferris wheel ride, they made their way to a retro-looking photo booth tucked in a corner of the amusement park.

"Let's take some pictures," Levi suggested, a playful glint in his eyes.

Khynzy looked hesitant for a moment, but then nodded. "Alright, let's do it."

As they crammed into the tiny photo booth, Levi helped

Blue onto his lap, making sure the little one could be seen in the frame.

"Ready?" Levi asked, meeting Khynzy's eyes in the mirror. She nodded, and he inserted the coins to start the session.

The first flash popped, capturing all three of them in a standard family pose: Levi's arm around Khynzy and Blue's little hand waving at the camera.

"For the next one, let's make wacky faces!" Levi exclaimed. Blue giggled in anticipation. The second flash captured exaggerated smiles, wide eyes, and tongues sticking out.

The third flash was reserved for Blue's favourite superhero pose. Blue flexed his little muscles, pretending to fly, while Levi and Khynzy pointed at him, their faces filled with mock astonishment.

"Last one," Levi said softly, locking eyes with Khynzy for just a moment. As the final flash prepared to burst, he swiftly leaned over and gently kissed Khynzy's lips. Blue, still on his lap, clapped his tiny hands together, delighted by the unexpected action.

The curtain drew back, and the machine whirred; Levi chose the option for two copies. Moments later, two identical strips of glossy photos were dispensed. He took one strip and handed the other to Khynzy.

Levi examined the images: a beautiful encapsulation of their day—fun, surprising, and emotionally charged. The last photo was especially telling: him kissing Khynzy, the surprised yet soft look in her eyes, and Blue clapping, completely unaware of the complex emotions between his parents.

Lunch followed—a delightful mess of amusement park staples. Hot dogs, waffles, and cotton candy that Blue was all too excited to make disappear. "Watch, Papa!" he exclaimed, stuffing the cotton candy into his mouth.

"Oh, wow! You made it disappear!" Levi chuckled, his eyes

meeting Khynzy's once more. She smiled, and although it didn't reach her eyes like it once did, it was a start.

As the afternoon sun began to dip, "One last ride," Levi announced.

"The spaceship!" Blue yelled, his eyes lighting up at the sight of the rocket-shaped ride.

As they began to exit the ride, Levi found himself whispering to Khynzy, "Today was perfect," his eyes searching hers for a sign.

"Almost perfect," she replied softly, her gaze holding his. In that moment, among the complexities of their past and the uncertainties of their future, Levi thought he saw a glimmer of hope.

Carrying that sense of hope, they left the theme park and made their next stop. They stepped into the quiet elegance of a high-end jewellery store, the cool, air-conditioned oasis providing a soothing contrast to the day's earlier excitement. The refined surroundings, with their soft lighting and exquisite displays, spoke of timeless luxury.

Today was significant for Levi, marking what he felt was a pivotal moment in their ever-evolving relationship. They were here to pick up the matching watches they had once exchanged as a testament to their love. These timepieces, now polished to a shine after professional cleaning, were laden with memories of a chapter filled with love and promise.

As the attendant delicately handed them their watches, Levi's heart was awash with nostalgia and a silent longing. These watches, symbols of their shared past, resonated with stories of joy and sorrow. Slipping his watch back on, Levi felt its familiar weight as a silent beacon of hope – a hope for a second chance at the love they once nurtured.

In that moment of reflection, Levi's gaze was drawn to a display of pendants. The idea struck him – a pendant, or perhaps two, would make a perfect gift for their son. It would be a symbol of their bond, a token from a father to his son, carrying the message that even though paths might diverge, the connection remained unbreakable. Levi studied the array of pendants in the display case. A silver astronaut, a rocket ship, and a pendant shaped like the letter 'B' caught his eye. Perfect for Blue, their young son, who was fascinated by the cosmos.

"Papa, astro!" Blue's tiny fingers tapped the glass to point at the astronaut pendant, his eyes wide with excitement.

Levi crouched down to Blue's level. "The astronaut, the rocket, and the 'B' for Blue. What do you think about getting all three, buddy?"

Blue clapped his hands in sheer joy. "All three, yay!"

"Looks like he'll have quite the collection," Khynzy said, smiling at the duo.

Just as Levi moved to approach the counter to make the purchase, a troubling thought invaded his mind. *Just a bit closer to the counter, and I can grab some jewellery while the car rams in.*

Levi tried to sway the man's intent but realised the determination was too strong to be influenced, and the man seemed to be waiting for another robber who might be ramming a car into the store.

"Zee, we need to go. Now." Levi's voice was a low but urgent whisper to Khynzy. He could hear thoughts of malice swirling in the air around them, closing in.

Khynzy felt a sudden surge in Levi's emotional state but couldn't see his aura to understand what was happening.

Just as Khynzy was about to ask why, the room erupted into mayhem. The screeching of tires was immediately followed by the horrific crash of a car smashing through the storefront window. Glass and sparkly jewels rained down like deadly confetti, and people screamed, diving for cover.

Auras around clouded with fear and dread. Khynzy

looked at Blue, her motherly instincts on high alert. She couldn't see Blue's aura, just like how she couldn't see Levi's.

Levi turned to swoop Blue into his arms, intending to use his body as a human shield to protect his son and Khynzy. But just as he bent down, a man lunged from the chaos, grabbing Blue in a chokehold and pulling him away. Levi reacted on instinct, lunging for the gun the man brandished. He managed to grip the robber's hand, steering the gun away from Khynzy and Blue.

The atmosphere was electric, time seeming to slow as Levi grappled with the man. Just when he thought he could overpower him, a gunshot sounded before he felt the searing pain rip through his side, causing him to crumple to the floor.

Seizing the moment, security swiftly apprehended the robbers. But as they did, Levi started to lose consciousness. As the edges of his vision began to blur, Levi locked eyes with Blue, who had been released and was now in Khynzy's arms.

"Papa!" Blue's voice mixed with terror and worry.

Khynzy, her eyes wide with fear, clung tightly to Blue. Paramedics rushed in, swift and professional, stabilising Levi with practised hands before lifting him onto a stretcher. A chilling realisation washed over her—she couldn't bear the thought of losing Levi, not now, not ever.

"We're going with him," Khynzy told the paramedic, her voice tinged with a newfound determination.

As they climbed into the ambulance, Blue snuggled against her while she reached out to hold Levi's limp hand. His palm felt cold, his strong fingers unresponsive.

Blue sobbed, his little hands tugging at Levi's shirt, trying to wake him up. "Why isn't Papa waking up?"

Khynzy held Blue close, struggling to find reassuring words amidst her own fear. "He's going to be okay. The doctors will do their best to help him."

As the ambulance sirens wailed into the night, Khynzy's grip tightened on Levi's hand. In that fraught moment, filled with uncertainty and fear, she knew that their love—complex, strained, but unbreakable—would be their anchor through whatever lay ahead.

60

A Life Without Levi

The wail of the ambulance siren filled the air as it sped through the city streets. Inside, the atmosphere was tense. Khynzy sat beside Blue, who clutched her hand tightly, his eyes wide with fear and confusion. "Mama, is Papa going to be okay?" he asked in a quivering voice.

Khynzy, her eyes moist with unshed tears, squeezed his hand. "I hope so, sweetheart," she whispered, trying to mask her fear.

Beside them, Levi lay on the stretcher, his breathing shallow. The paramedics were vigilant, monitoring his vitals closely, especially mindful of the gunshot wound on his side. They had done their best to stabilize the wound, but the urgency was palpable.

Suddenly, the heart monitor emitted a prolonged, high-pitched beep – Levi had flatlined. The paramedic in charge sprang into action. "He's in asystole!" he announced, beginning chest compressions with precise force, careful to avoid aggravating Levi's wound.

"Prepare epinephrine," another paramedic instructed, swiftly drawing up the medication. Khynzy watched, her heart in her throat, as the team worked tirelessly. Blue buried his face in her side, overwhelmed by the scene unfolding.

Despite the cramped confines of the ambulance, the paramedics moved with practised efficiency, their actions a well-rehearsed dance against time. After a tense minute that felt like an eternity, the heart monitor suddenly emitted a steady beep – Levi's heart was beating again.

Relief washed over Khynzy, though she knew they weren't out of danger yet. The paramedic met her eyes, a mix of professional calm and empathy in his gaze. "We've got his heart beating again, but he's not out of the woods. We'll be at the hospital soon, where he can receive more comprehensive care."

As the ambulance continued its urgent journey, Khynzy held Blue closer, whispering words of comfort. The renewed beeping of the heart monitor was a fragile thread of hope, a promise that where there was life, there was still a chance.

The ambulance screeched to a halt at the hospital's emergency entrance. The back doors swung open immediately, revealing the urgent bustle of the ER. Paramedics, with swift and practised movements, unloaded Levi's stretcher. His condition remained critical, the gunshot wound on his side a stark contrast against the sterile white sheets.

Khynzy followed closely, Blue's hand gripped tightly in hers, as they navigated the practised environment of the ER. The paramedics wheeled Levi through the sliding doors that led to the treatment area, moving with a speed that mirrored the urgency of the situation.

As the doors closed behind Levi, cutting him off from their view, Khynzy and Blue were gently guided by a nurse to a nearby waiting area. The nurse offered them reassuring words, but Khynzy's eyes remained fixed on the doors, behind which the medical team was now fighting to save Levi's life. In the waiting area, the tension was palpable, a mix of hope and fear hanging in the air as they awaited news.

Desperation gripped her as she dialled Stella. "Stella, Levi's been shot. I'm at the hospital. I need you." She tried to sound strong, but her voice trembled.

A trauma surgeon soon approached. "We've stabilised him," he said gravely, "but we need to get that bullet out. It's dangerously close to vital organs. Also, he has a rare blood type: AB negative."

Khynzy knew just the person. She quickly called Owen. "Owen, Levi's in trouble. We need you."

Owen arrived in what felt like mere moments, his face lined with worry. Blue approached him, his voice quivering, "Uncle Owen, please help Papa."

Owen knelt down in front of Blue, meeting his gaze with a softness. "I'll do everything I can, kiddo," he reassured. Standing back up, he looked at Khynzy with determination, "I'm ready. Just tell me where to go."

Guided by a nurse, Owen was quickly ushered to a preparation room for blood donation.

As Owen was led away, the entrance to the waiting area slid open to reveal Stella, her face a mask of concern. Upon seeing Khynzy's eyes brim with tears, Stella immediately rushed forward, pulling her friend into a warm embrace. "I don't know what to do, Stella," Khynzy choked out, her voice muffled against Stella's shoulder.

Stella tightened her hold, offering reassuring words. "It's going to be okay. We're here for you."

After a while, Owen emerged from the preparation room, his face a shade paler but his determination unwavering. He approached Khynzy. "Did it help? How's he doing?"

Khynzy gave a weary smile. "Thank you, Owen. They moved Levi to the operating room. The surgeons are working on him now. Your blood might just save his life."

Owen glanced at the door leading to the operating room.

"He's tough. He'll pull through. And if my blood can help, then it's the least I can do."

Stella handed Owen a bottle of water. "You should sit down and rest."

Nodding in appreciation, Owen sat next to Blue, patting the boy's head softly as he sipped water.

The long hours that followed were agonising. The surgeon eventually emerged with a tired smile. "He's stable. The bullet is out." But Levi hadn't woken up.

As night settled, Khynzy was lost in her thoughts, the rhythmic beeping of Levi's heart monitor a grim metronome to her reflections. They'd had their ups and downs, their shared moments of joy and pain. The weight of the past, combined with the looming uncertainty of the present, pressed down on her. She felt the profound realisation that a world without Levi was not a world she wanted or could bear. The thought was overwhelming, and tears streamed down her face.

Blue, curled up on a nearby chair, murmured softly in his sleep, "Papa."

Ever the pillar of strength, Stella gently squeezed Khynzy's shoulder, urging her to rest.

But Khynzy couldn't. She whispered softly to the unconscious Levi, "Please come back to us."

61

Awakening and Healing

Levi's eyes fluttered open, adjusting to the glaring light of the hospital room. When he saw Khynzy seated beside him, her hand intertwined with his, a wave of comfort and relief washed over him. In that moment, he realised something profound: the bravery he had shown wasn't some abstract notion of courage; it had been fuelled by the immediate need to protect Khynzy and Blue.

"You're awake," Khynzy whispered, her voice tinged with relief and unspoken emotion. She had come to understand that she couldn't fathom a life without Levi, especially after he had risked so much for them.

"Hey," Levi rasped, feeling parched.

"Here," Khynzy offered, lifting a cup of water to his lips for a sip. "How are you feeling?"

"Like I got shot," he quipped, regretting it instantly as her expression winced. "Sorry, bad joke."

With a deep breath, Levi finally asked, "Is there a chance for us, Zee?"

Khynzy locked eyes with him, her heart racing. "Let's focus on you getting well first. Then we can talk about it, I promise."

Just then, Blue stirred. Upon realising his papa was awake, he shouted, "Papa! You're awake!" and cautiously hugged him.

"Careful, sweetheart," Khynzy cautioned. "Don't touch Papa's wound; it might hurt him."

Blue carefully planted a kiss near the bandage. "Better, Papa?"

Emotionally touched, Levi chuckled. "Much better, thanks, buddy."

Levi smiled, hugging him back carefully to avoid his wound. "Missed me?"

"Super missed you, Papa. Were you sleeping 'cause you were super tired?"

"No, buddy. Papa was hurt, but I'm getting better now."

"You're my hero, Papa!" Blue exclaimed, admiration filling his young eyes.

"I'm glad you think so, little man," Levi said, his eyes meeting Khynzy's for a moment.

With a shift in mood, Blue's excitement bubbled up as he held up a tablet. "Oh, I want to show you something!" He tapped on the screen, displaying a picture of Khynzy, noticeably pregnant. With a playful and clever glint in his eyes, Blue asked, "Can you find me in the picture, Papa?"

Levi, taken aback, took a moment before replying, "Were you in Mama's tummy here?"

Blue nodded excitedly. "Yes! I was like an astronaut."

Levi chuckled, "Always so imaginative, aren't you? That reminds me, I promised to give you a 'B,' a rocket ship, and an astronaut pendant, right?"

Blue's eyes widened in excitement but then softened as he looked at both his parents. "I think all I need is my Papa and Mama. But gifts are super cool too!"

As they sat there, the room seemed to expand, making way for the raw emotion and newfound understanding that filled it.

☙

Later in the evening, as Levi lay in the hospital bed, he looked over at his son Blue. The boy was curled up beside him, sleeping soundly and peacefully.

Khynzy stood by the window, staring out before finally turning to look at Levi. In that moment, both were acutely aware of their unique exceptions: Levi couldn't hear Khynzy's thoughts, and Khynzy couldn't see Levi's aura. The silence was thick with all the things that their abilities had never let them share.

"Zee, you know what'll help with my recovery?" Levi finally broke the quiet.

Khynzy approached, pulling a chair close to the bed. "You want something?"

"Yeah," Levi said softly, locking eyes with Khynzy. "A kiss."

Time seemed to pause as Khynzy leaned in. The air between them grew thick with anticipation, like the charged atmosphere before a storm. As their lips finally met, Khynzy felt a jolt of electricity, as if they'd both touched a live wire at the same moment.

Levi's lips were softer than Khynzy had remembered, a surprising contrast to the hard resolve often seen in his eyes. She felt a swarm of butterflies take flight in her stomach. Her aura, a mixture of red and pink, seemed to ripple and swirl as if catching up on years missed.

For Levi, the moment their lips touched, it was as if he had found the missing code to a complex algorithm, unlocking a rush of emotions that had been compiling for years. A wave of warmth radiated from the point of contact, filling him with a sense of comfort and rightness.

Just as Khynzy began to pull back, savouring the ticklish sensation that lingered on her lips, a feeling of urgency gripped Levi. Afraid of letting the moment slip through his fingers, his hand reached up instinctively to cradle the back of

Khynzy's head. The tactile sensation of Khynzy's hair beneath his fingers was grounding, a physical anchor to the emotional storm brewing within him. The touch sent another current of electricity down Khynzy's spine, amplifying the butterflies into a full-blown whirlwind.

As their lips met again, Levi felt as if he were soaring. His heart pounded in his chest, not from fear or anxiety but from the sheer exhilaration of being so close to Khynzy, of tasting and feeling her again in a way he'd only allowed himself to dream about.

In that moment, every sense was heightened, every emotion magnified. Their mouths moved in sync now, as if each had found the perfect counterbalance in the other. Five years of longing, regret, and missed opportunities funnelled into that kiss as if trying to make up for all the lost time in a single, electrifying connection.

When they finally broke the kiss, Khynzy looked into Levi's eyes, a mixture of relief and admonishment on her face. "Don't you ever do something that dangerous again."

Feeling warmth spread through his heart, Levi grinned. "Worried about me now?"

Khynzy sighed, the corner of her mouth twitching upward. "I've never stopped being concerned about you."

Levi's soft whisper barely filled the dimly lit hospital room. "Zee, there's something I've wanted to ask since you came back." His eyes earnestly sought hers. Gently caressing Blue's hair, Khynzy returned his gaze, and a quiet "What is it, Lev?" slipped past her lips.

The vulnerability in his eyes was palpable as he found the courage to ask, "Have you been with anyone else since we broke up?" Khynzy's eyes welled up, glistening in the low light, yet she held her composure. "No, I haven't," she whispered, her voice steady yet soft.

Khynzy's gaze moved to Blue, then back to Levi, her voice

barely audible. "Have you?" Levi exhaled a relief-filled sigh, responding gently, "No, I haven't."

Trembling slightly, Khynzy confided, "But my friends said... men need... Levi, are you being honest with me?" His hand found hers. "I am, Zee. I promise you. I had my lonely moments, but I..." he paused, then continued softly, "I took care of it myself, you might say. But even in those moments of solitude, it was always you in my thoughts."

As their fingers gently entwined, he whispered, "I've never stopped loving you. Every moment, every day... it was always you, Zee."

Emotion shimmered in Khynzy's eyes as she softly spoke, "Lev, I was so scared to ask. Scared that you might have moved on, that you might have found comfort in someone else's arms." His reassuring whisper came, "I couldn't. My heart couldn't find a home anywhere else but with you."

They shared a moment of silent understanding, while Blue, blissfully unaware of the emotional exchange between his parents, continued to sleep peacefully beside them.

After a pause, Khynzy's expression softened further. "I also owe you an apology, Lev. You know, about my parents... I blamed you for something that... well, while you could have tried harder, you didn't have any bad intentions. And back then, you were just a kid. It wasn't fair of me to put that on you."

Hearing those words, Levi felt a weight lift off his shoulders, one he'd carried for far too long. "That's the biggest regret of my life, you know. I wish every day that I could've done more. But hearing you say that... it means more than you can imagine."

Khynzy nodded, her eyes glistening. "Let's just promise to move forward, for us and Blue. No more regrets."

Their eyes locked, a universe of feelings passing between them. Slowly, Khynzy leaned in, her eyes never leaving his.

Levi, too, moved closer, until their breaths mingled and the world around them seemed to pause.

It was a kiss laced with the pain of the past and the hope of the future. When they parted a few moments later, their foreheads rested together, sharing the same air, the same space, intimately close.

Levi's voice was a soft, vulnerable whisper against her lips. "So, Zee, does this mean from now on, I don't need to take care of 'it' myself?"

Khynzy's eyes, a mixture of emotions, met his as a gentle smile formed on her lips. "Lev," she whispered back, "you'll find out once your wound is healed and you get discharged."

A playful glint sparkled through his gaze. "Maybe I should talk to the doctor, see if we can speed up the healing process a bit?" he teased, his voice light despite the emotional heaviness of their exchange.

A soft chuckle escaped her, and she shook her head, caressing his cheek tenderly. "No shortcuts, mister," Khynzy gently chided. "Healing needs time. And as for 'it', your patience, all this while and a little longer, means everything to me."

Levi gently cradled her face, eyes reflecting deep, unwavering love. "Zee," he murmured, "for you, for us, I'd wait an eternity. You and Blue are everything. I'm not going anywhere."

62

A New Beginning

Levi had been planning this day for weeks. As much as he could read the darker intentions in people's minds, he could never penetrate the beautiful mystery of Khynzy's thoughts. Nor could she see his aura. That unique situation made their relationship even more magical.

Tonight had an air of significance that transcended any ordinary evening. Their journey together had been fraught with so many highs and lows that it could fill volumes— moments of love eclipsed by loss, punctuated by brushes with death. If their life were a book, one might wonder why fate seemed so set on testing them with a series of unfortunate events. But here they were, standing on the precipice of a future they could shape into anything they wanted.

Levi had meticulously planned for this night, down to the last detail. Khynzy was led to believe that their friend Stella had enthusiastically agreed to babysit Blue. She didn't know that her son was practically bursting with excitement over the "super special surprise for Mama" that his dad had confided in him about.

For Levi, this evening wasn't just another date night; it was a promise, a pledge to face whatever trials lay ahead hand in hand, always. And as they stepped out, leaving their son giggling with Stella, he felt a sense of completeness. It was as though all the scattered pieces of their intricate puzzle were finally falling into place. Tonight, he would make sure of it.

Levi wore a tailored black suit with a silver tie, and Khynzy was radiant in a flowing navy blue gown. Levi took Khynzy to the rooftop restaurant where they'd shared their first kiss. Tonight, they were the only patrons. He had arranged for the other glass domes and tables to be removed, providing them complete privacy. The setting sun bathed the city in a soft, orange glow. The glass dome that had been part of their first kiss was still there, adorned with tasteful arrangements of roses and lilies, a chandelier, and fairy lights that twinkled in the waning light.

As they arrived at their table, Khynzy looked around, visibly impressed. "You did all this?"

"I wanted tonight to be perfect," Levi said, guiding her to a plush sofa where they could sit side by side, just like before.

They enjoyed a lovely dinner, and as dessert was served, Levi looked into Khynzy's eyes. "Zee, we've been through a lot. Highs, lows, joys, and sorrows. I can't imagine going through any of it with anyone else."

Khynzy's eyes twinkled, but before she could say anything, Levi continued.

"You can see auras, the colours of emotion. But for some reason, you can't see mine, and I think that's the universe telling us we should fill in the colours ourselves, write our own destiny."

As he spoke, he reached into his pocket and pulled out a small box. Opening it, he revealed a diamond ring that captured the room's light in a dazzling display. "Zee, will you marry me?"

Time seemed to pause. Khynzy's eyes filled with joyful

tears. After what felt like an eternity but was only a few seconds, she finally spoke.

"Yes," she whispered, her face illuminated by a radiant smile.

Levi carefully slid the ring onto her finger, its sparkle a testament to the bright future they were about to embark upon. Then, as if drawn by an invisible force, their lips met in a kiss that sealed their commitment to each other. At that moment, they both felt an overwhelming sense of completeness, assured that their love story was one for the ages, coloured in shades and hues uniquely their own.

Just then, Blue came rushing in, dressed in a little grey vest and trousers, looking just like a mini version of his dad.

"Mama, Papa, what's happening?" he exclaimed, rushing over.

Khynzy bent down to be at eye level with him. "Blue, Papa asked me a very important question, and I said yes."

Blue looked puzzled for a moment, and then his eyes widened. "You're getting married?"

"That's right, buddy," Levi confirmed, lifting his son into his arms. "How do you feel about that?

Blue's eyes sparkled. "Best news ever!"

Blue hugged both of them tightly. "I love it! Oh, Papa, the colours around you are bright and pink and gold!"

Khynzy and Levi exchanged a surprised glance. "You can see them?" Khynzy asked, her voice tinged with astonishment.

"Those colours mean love and happiness, Blue," Khynzy explained, gently touching her son's cheek.

With Blue still in his arms, Levi pulled Khynzy into a warm embrace. "You know, this is the most colourful and happiest my world has ever been."

"And mine too," Khynzy whispered, as they stood there, wrapped in an aura of love, the colours of their emotions painting a future full of endless possibility.

Thank You For Reading Luminance & Resonance!

Dear Reader,

I sincerely hope you enjoyed journeying through the pages of Luminance and Resonance. It means the world to me that you chose to spend your time in the world I've created.

If you enjoyed the adventure, I have a small favour to ask: would you consider sharing your thoughts with a review? Your feedback not only helps me grow as a writer but also assists other readers in finding books they'll love.

Leaving a review doesn't have to be lengthy—a few sentences about what you enjoyed would be immensely appreciated. You can share your thoughts on platforms where books are discussed and sold.

Every single review makes a significant impact and helps more than you might realise. Again, thank you for your support—it truly means the world to me.

Wishing you all the best in your reading adventures,

Lhyndzy

Find Me Online

Join me online to explore the world of my writing and connect over shared passions:

- Website: Visit lhyndzy.com to learn more about my work, explore upcoming projects, and enjoy exclusive content.
- Email: Feel free to reach out at admin@lhyndzy.com with your thoughts or inquiries.
- Instagram: Follow my journey on Instagram at lhyndzy.writes for updates and behind-the-scenes content.
- TikTok: Join me on TikTok at lhyndzy.writes to enjoy creative snippets and book trailers.

I look forward to connecting with you and sharing my literary adventures!